Recipe for Love

Veronika Sophia Robinson

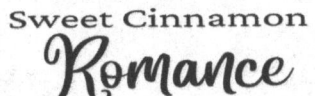

For my sister, Heidi.
I love you, and I love your vegetable lasagne!

About Veronika Sophia Robinson

Veronika spent her childhood on a 700-acre horse stud in rural Australia, and her teenage years immersed in romance novels. They provided just the antidote to boring schooldays and tedious exams. Instead of doing homework, she was being romanced by tall, dark, fictional men...that is, until she could hear her mother walking up the hallway to her bedroom. And then, her secret lover was shoved beneath her textbooks while she pretended to studiously examine the theory of how to dissect a frog. Talk about going from princes to frogs! She was thrown out of biology class for drawing hearts. Love hearts!

She met her husband Paul—a prince, not a frog—when living in New Zealand, and they moved in together the day after their first date. It was 'I've known you forever' at first sight. Their love story is a rom-com; she's the rom, he's the com. Veronika has been a marriage celebrant since 1995, when her first daughter just started kicking inside her belly.

She lives a charmed life in the heart of the Cumbrian countryside, in the north of England.

Veronika's passions include barefoot gardening, cooking, psychological astrology, reading and writing, walking in the woods, and being with her family and friends. www.veronikarobinson.com

Recipe for Love
© Veronika Sophia Robinson
© Cover illustration by Heidi Harbers
Published by Sweet Cinnamon Romance
An imprint of Starflower Press
ISBN: 978-0-9931586-7-4
St. Valentine's Day 2023

A CIP catalogue record for this book is available from the British Library.

Published by Sweet Cinnamon Romance, an imprint of Starflower Press www.starflowerpress.com

Books by the same author at www.veronikarobinson.com

Sweet Cinnamon Romances
are contemporary love stories set around the world.
Cinnamon symbolises abundance, protection and passion.

Limetree Hollow

Beau Candler wasn't sure if it was intuition, or gut instinct, or just that he knew the reputation of slimy Keith McVeigh far too well. When he saw the rusty tractor driving ridiculously fast up the pot-holed dirt track toward the old Mason homestead at Limetree Hollow, his stomach jarred. Something didn't feel right. There was no logical reason for Keith to be driving there.

Beau had already heard that Jack's granddaughter, Mahalia Mason, inherited the place, and that she was moving in—small-town gossip travels fast—but he couldn't understand why she'd invite a no-gooder like Keith up there. No, something definitely wasn't right. Beau wouldn't trust Keith with a cattle dog, so he could hardly trust him to keep his grubby hands off a young woman from the city. A beautiful young woman, if memory served him correctly. She must be what, about twenty six now? Beau's heart pounded even harder when he recalled the last time he saw Mahalia.

Back then, she was seventeen years old—a month shy of eighteen, she told him more than once—and riding her grandfather's pony up the mountain. They met by the clearing on Hallow's Ridge, and he could see in her eyes that she was smitten with him. They talked comfortably for an hour or so, as they rode down the mountain, side by side. Beau told himself, repeatedly, that she was nothing more than jailbait, and he knew it was in both their interests not to express how attractive he found her.

As Beau drove his Jaguar along the bumpy, rocky road to her house, cursing at the untold damage it was doing and wondering why he didn't take the Jeep, he wondered if she was still attractive. Was she seeing anyone? Was she married? *Stop it*, he told himself. Beau put his thoughts straight. He was going to her house: and it *was* her house now, to check that she was safe, not to see what she looked like! But his thoughts kept leading him astray. If he was honest with himself, he'd been looking for a good reason to run into her.

There was Keith's tractor, edged up by the front verandah. No sign of him or Mahalia. That was her name, wasn't it? Suddenly he couldn't think straight. Of course that was her name. But then again, maybe he'd had her name wrong all these years. Something exotic, was all he remembered. Oh yes, he sighed, *exotic*; with long legs and fiery copper-red hair which hung in never-ending ringlets down the entire length of her back.

Beau found himself hoping that she hadn't cut off her long locks; he shook his head in disbelief that he was feeling so protective of her. What was going on? The last thing he needed in his life was to be distracted by a beautiful woman.

The motor of the Jaguar idled for a moment, and then Beau turned the engine off. He quickly walked onto the verandah, and was about to knock when he heard loud voices coming from the barn. Instinctively, he headed back across the yard, quickening his step, and stood near the stable doors. It took him a few seconds to register what he was witnessing: Keith had Mahalia cornered: she looked terrified, like a rabbit in headlights.

'Leave me alone!' she yelled, her face as red as her hair.

Beau didn't know whether to laugh at the image of the female devil with a fiery mane who was brandishing a fork, or to rescue her.

Then she raised the pitch fork up towards Keith's head ready to attack.

'Get out, or I'll put this thing through your head!' she warned him. And with one quick movement, Keith had the handle of the fork in his hands, and then threw it behind him as he lunged forward towards her, throwing her onto the straw-covered ground.

'What the hell do you think you're doing?' Beau roared, never feeling angrier in his life. 'Get the hell off her, and get out of here before I put that fork through you myself!'

Keith, shamefaced, scrambled to his feet. The last thing he'd expected was to have anyone turn up at the old farm.

'Get out!' Beau's voice thundered across the barn. 'We'll be pressing charges!'

Keith limped out, and shaking his head in shock, moved quickly. Once he limbered up the old tractor, it scooted down the road.

'I'm quite capable of looking after myself,' Mahalia insisted, brushing straw from her jeans, and then walked swiftly towards the house studiously avoided eye contact.

Beau Candler had been the object of her teenage fantasies, and this was not the reunion she had planned. No, in her mind, they'd sip wine on the verandah and watch the stars. But here she was, covered in straw, hair dishevelled and face flushed. Not the image she wanted to project after eight long years. Beau couldn't possibly find her attractive when she was fuming.

'I can see that,' he said, a slow smile easing across his face and bringing light to his eyes.

Despite her declarations of independence, she was shaking.

Beau reached for her hand. 'Come on, you need a cup of tea.'

Mahalia was grateful, so very grateful, for his intervention; she wanted to tell him as much, but the electricity when he touched her catapulted Mahalia to a wholly new place where she'd never been before. At that moment, she wasn't sure if she shouldn't be more scared of the effect he was having on her than the one low-life McVeigh had.

'Settling in well then?' he chuckled, aware that he'd just rescued her from a situation he couldn't bear thinking about, and trying to lighten the mood.

'Still unpacking,' she said, and as they walked through the front door, all Beau could see was chaos. His worst nightmare: things out of order.

'I can, however, make you a coffee or tea,' she offered, taking a moment to eye up her knight in shining armour. As her pulse quickened, Mahalia realised that she didn't remember him being *this* handsome.

Though his muscles were lean, and his strong jawline had two days of growth, she was rather terrified at the primal surges pulsing through her red-blooded veins.

'That'd be great. Whatever you're having.'

Beau watched her as she moved around the kitchen. The house may have been filled with unpacked boxes, but the kitchen already looked like a jungle: pots filled with herbs and plants, and vases of flowers lined the benches and window sills. Still shaking, he could see that she was in no position to make anything.

'You sit, I'll make it.'

The look of relief in her eyes didn't escape him.

Mahalia pointed him in the direction of the tea cupboard. While Beau made a cafetiere of strong coffee, he heated up some milk on the stove.

'So, tell me, have you moved in for good?' he asked, finally passing her a cup.

'The plan was to stay for the Summer and photograph for the cookery book that I wrote last year, but...'

'You're too scared to stay now, aren't you?' Beau looked concerned. 'I can't promise that idiot won't be back. I can have a word to the sheriff, if you like?'

Beau studied her as she looked down into her coffee, as if she were reading tea leaves; as if she could forecast her future. But he wondered if all she could see was a fear of that man turning up whenever he wanted.

'It's probably best if I just go back home.'

And as soon as she said those words—"go back home"—Beau Candler thought: *over my dead body*. There was no way she was leaving her grandfather's old home this time. Not now that she wasn't seventeen years old. Not now. Not now that she was a ...*woman*. Somehow, she was even more beautiful than he remembered. And he had thought about her often over the years: the way she laughed, or tossed her hair over her shoulders. They way she insisted on always picking posies of wildflowers. Beau remembered how she used to sing the same song all the time: *Swallow*, by the Wailin' Jennys. But mostly what he remembered was that when he looked into her eyes he could see hope and happiness. It was confusing, and many times he tried to dismiss such thoughts. She's a girl, he told himself.

A girl! But that girl from the city had big dreams and a big heart, and her zest for life left a place in his heart. It stole a secret corner that he kept all to himself. It was a silly fantasy, and he made a determined effort to rid his mind of any such dreams.

'Why did you come here to photograph?' Beau asked, trying to keep the conversation casual.

'I loved coming here as a child, and especially as a teenager. It was my sanctuary from the tough times of having to sit exams and make difficult choices about what to do with the rest of my life.'

Beau knew that he wasn't what she came to the countryside for, and that any temptations would be nothing but a time-wasting distraction from her mission.

'Granddad spoiled me rotten, and I could ride the horses for hours. I had so much freedom here. I always felt safe. Ironic, huh?'

'You should feel safe here! Damn it!' And the sound of his fist thumping on the table made them both jump. 'I'm sorry, I didn't mean to scare you.'

'I'm a bit on edge. I came here for a taste of that freedom. I knew it would give me the space to photograph my recipes inside and outside in natural light, and to tap into my creative muse at all hours of the day. I left my café in someone else's hands, so I could just focus on this. If I stayed back home, I'd be worrying about the café, and dropping in to check on things. Out here, I knew I wouldn't be so tempted. Don't have much choice now, though...' and her words trailed off in frustration and desperation. 'I've been planning this for months! I only arrived yesterday, and now I'm going home. I'm so angry!'

Beau tried hard to repress the smile that was forming on his lips. Did she have to look so darned gorgeous when she was angry? Mahalia tossed her copper hair over her shoulders, and stood up. Beau would do anything to hold her; anything to make up for all the years that they *could* have been together.

'Thank you for arriving when you did today. Really. Thank you.'

Beau stood up, too, and was close beside her. They were face to face, breathing in the warmth of each other's breath. Strangers, and yet somehow like old friends: new, and familiar. Mahalia smelled of fresh garden herbs, and Spring sunshine. It was ironic that a grubby old farmer had brought them together this day. Neither of them wanted to part. Who was going to give in first? A kiss was inevitable. It had to be. They were magnetised by each other's eyes. Beau moved first, taking a deep breath, then carried the cups to the sink.

Such a simple, helpful action, and yet she felt like someone had just slapped her across the face. Mahalia stood there, reeling. What the hell just happened? Didn't he find her attractive? Why did he walk away like that? How could she have confused attraction for…what did she confuse it with? Surely he felt it too? Mahalia was dumbstruck.

'I guess since you've not really unpacked anything, it's just a matter of the removalists coming in and collecting everything again?' Beau asked, his back to her while washing cups. It was all he could do to contain his urges. If he followed his desires, he'd swoop down and kiss her. Beau focused on washing each cup thoroughly, then grabbed a towel to dry them off; stalling for time until he had to turn around and face her again.

'Yeah.'

When Beau finally turned around, he looked into her deep smoky green eyes, and said, 'Men like Keith are always waiting to prey on women who are alone. Have you got anyone you can invite to stay here with you?'

It was obvious that she was touched by his kindness, and she laughed a little. 'No one who can take three months off their job!'

Beau raised his eyebrows in acknowledgement. Of course not. Real people had real jobs. Not everyone in the world had his level of freedom and income to just up sticks and make that sort of change to their life.

Beau started towards the door, and then stood looking out across the yard. At six foot three, his silhouette filled the doorway. In frustration, he hit the door with his fist, and turned abruptly to look at her.

'I can't walk away from here knowing that scum is making you leave. It's not right,' he said furiously. Beau looked over to the barn, then turned to face her. 'I've got an idea. My place has a kitchen I hardly use. Why don't you stay at the manor to photograph the rest of your book? And… and if you want to come back here for outside photos, I can come with you. That way, I know you'll be safe. So, what do you think? Have we got a deal?'

The words had hardly left his mouth, when his brain kicked in wondering just who gave him permission to do something so crazy, so irresponsible. If she was in his house, for even a night, there'd be no telling what would happen. Their close encounter just a few minutes earlier was proof of that. And right now, he wanted to hoist her up on the kitchen table, with her long legs wrapped around him tightly. He wanted to… Beau groaned softly and wondered if she could read his mind; a tinge of colour rushed to his unshaven cheeks.

So taken by his captivating smile, she barely heard what he said. Maybe she was imagining his incredibly kind offer? Mahalia wanted to jump at the offer, especially if it meant being anywhere near the magnificent Beau Candler. In that moment, she searched frantically for the words, the right words…but where were they? All she knew was that three months in close proximity to him would be the end of her. It would undo the life she knew.

'Beau, that is incredibly generous, but, why? What do you get out of it?'

'Someone has to eat that food, right?' he laughed, and just the sound of his gravelly tones eased them both. It was as if Keith McVeigh hadn't even been there that day. All fear evaporated.

'Agreed?' he asked, feeling rather pleased with himself. She had to say yes, surely? And he hoped, with all his heart, that she'd accept his offer.

'Seriously? Three months? You should know that I'm not easy to live with. I wake early, and cook like a fiend; I sing loudly to Bluegrass music, and I shower twice a day, and… I have to buy fresh flowers each week, and…'

'I think I can cope with that,' he smiled, easing his way into her heart just a little bit more. 'Sounds pretty low maintenance to me. Get what you need for tonight, and I'll send some of my workers over tomorrow with a truck to collect the rest. I'll wait in the car for you. Take your time. There's no rush.'

And there was that smile again. It was a mix of cheeky boy and rakishly handsome hero.

'Beau?' she said softly.

'Yeah?'

'Thank you.' And she'd never meant anything so much in her life. 'Thank you so much. For everything. For rescuing me, and for this invitation. You're so very kind.'

'My pleasure,' he said, feeling confident again.

Mahalia watched him walk to the car before remembering what she needed to do: she gathered an overnight bag and stuffed it with jeans, underwear, T-shirt, and nightie, her three cameras, and collected the box of organic vegetables from the kitchen bench, and her notebook. For a few long moments, she looked around the homestead—a place of so many happy meories—saddened to be leaving so soon, but overjoyed to be spending time in close proximity to Beau. It was a dream come true. A teenage girl's dream come true.

One last thing, she noted, as she picked up a glass jam jar filled with wildflowers: a posy of red native wild columbine that she'd plucked from the meadow earlier; and with her bag over her shoulder, headed out to the car with a skip in her step and a song in her heart. It was her favourite song: *Swallow*.

Red Maple Manor

They drove up the bumpy dirt road in silence, and as Beau pulled into the white-pebbled circular driveway of Red Maple Manor, Mahalia admired the long tree-lined drive, and the dozens of red maple trees.

'How long has the right of way to my granddad's been in place?' she asked.

'About three hundred years! I have to admit it's an annoyance, but your grandfather rarely had visitors, so I shouldn't complain. And besides, if it wasn't there, I wouldn't have known that Keith was paying you a visit.'

'A blessing, then?'

For both us, he thought to himself, acknowledging her with a warm smile.

'I'm sorry I wasn't there for your grandfather's funeral. I was overseas at the time. He was a good man. I've missed him around here.'

'Thank you. Yes, he was a good man. The best.'

Beau opened the car door for her, and reached out for her hand enjoying her smile as their eyes met.

This was either going to be the longest three months of her life, or the shortest. One thing was for sure: her eyes were going to treasure it. The man was devastatingly handsome, there was no arguing with that. But there was something else, too: a sadness behind his eyes, even when he was smiling. Like he didn't quite enjoy life; not fully, anyway. Perhaps she was just imagining it.

'When do you think you'll start cooking then?' he laughed, patting his rumbling tummy.

'Right now!' she said, raising her eyebrows at him

impatiently. 'It'll be a few hours, though, till you can eat. I'm making several dishes.'

Beau showed her through the vast walk-in pantry.

'This is bigger than my café! Holy Cow. Why do you have this when you're not a cook?'

'Well, you never know when you might get snowed in or want to throw a party,' he smiled. 'These cupboards along here contain all the cooking equipment. Tea towels are in here, cutlery is here, chopping boards are in here...'

'It's okay, Beau. I'll figure out where everything is.'

And in that moment, when she smiled so warmly, it was like when they'd met eight years ago, and he had to refrain from taking action. But it was different now, wasn't it? Mahalia was a woman, he was a man. Why shouldn't they see where their feelings and attraction went? They certainly didn't need anyone's permission.

'I have some errands to do,' Beau said. 'I'll be back in a few hours. Make yourself at home. Your bedroom is the first room on the right at the top of the staircase. It has an en suite, so you can take as many showers a day as you like and I'll never know; until the water bill comes in!' he laughed.

Not that he'd blink at any bill that came in the post. To say he was financially comfortable was an understatement.

'Here's my cellphone number if you need anything. I'll be back for 6pm. Anything you need while I'm in town, just ask.'

'Thanks.'

Mahalia watched as the Jaguar slowly wheeled out

of the driveway, crunching the small pebbles beneath its tyres. What an afternoon of mixed emotions. *Slime bucket*, she thought to herself when Keith McVeigh's grubby hands came back into her mind. And then, she found herself feeling just a smidgen of gratitude towards the lecherous farmer. If it wasn't for him, she wouldn't be standing in the most opulent kitchen she'd ever been in. Mahalia felt as if she was in a photo shoot for *House Beautiful* magazine. Three months cooking in here was going to be her version of heaven. Every day, looking out those white French windows across the circular driveway, and the Italian-style water fountain, to the fields beyond with Beau's Quarter horses. Mahalia pinched herself. This *was* real, wasn't it? She was standing in his kitchen, and he had invited her here to finish photographing her book? And she sighed at her turn of good fortune. Never in her wildest dreams did she imagine this. At best, she hoped their paths would cross and she could feast her eyes on his dashing smile. But here, now, in his home? For three months? She let out a squeal of joy.

Curiosity got the better of her, and Mahalia found herself wandering around the house. House? No, this was a mansion. *Maybe I'll need satellite navigation to find my way around?*

The reception area was larger than most houses she'd ever been in. The marble floor was adorned with Persian rugs. The first door she opened was on the left, and she entered a dining area. The mahogany table could easily seat fifty people. The views out the window were spectacular, and stretched across the Blue Ridge Mountains. What was a man like Beau Candler doing living here, in the middle of nowhere? A man who could take his pick of any woman he wanted, and yet, he'd made no mention of there being a lady of the house. Mahalia grabbed a fistful of her long ringleted hair, and scooped it into a loose bun on the top of her head, using strands of hair to tie it up.

Across the other side of the reception area, there was a vast lounge room with several three-seater sofas, in a bold red design. Despite the intensity of the colour, it worked well with the dark wooden beams and poles. Mahalia counted no less than twelve potted palms, about six-feet high. The wooden floorboards were wide, and covered in plush rugs in a matching holly-red colour. Above the huge open fireplace was a hand-carved, two-foot wide wooden mantlepiece. It took her a few moments to realise what was missing; what stopped it being a home. Mahalia noticed a distinct absence of photos. Sure, there was beautiful artwork on the walls, but nothing personal, nothing intimate, like a photo. Nothing that said: 'This is my life.' Perhaps other people wouldn't notice such a thing, but for Mahalia, who always had a camera nearby, it struck her as slightly odd. If a picture paints a thousand words, then no wonder she couldn't read him! *Where was the story of his life?*

For one last time, she surveyed the room; noticing the slide guitar and banjo in the corner. Then she made her way up the sweep of stairs. *First door on the right*, he said.

Mahalia reached for the handle, and wasn't entirely sure that it wasn't made from 24 carat gold. When she entered, her eyes opened wide in disbelief.

For a man who wasn't expecting visitors, the guest room sure did look inviting! There were spring flowers on the bedside table, the scent of honeysuckle greeting her as she sat on the bed. It was a king-sized four poster, decorated with soft silk georgette fabric over its canopy.

Mahalia walked over to the large glass doors, and stepped out onto the balcony, breathing in the late afternoon air coming off the mountains. The view was rather different on this side of the house. The first thing which caught her eye was the country church house, where her grandfather had been buried, and children playing in a field by the creek. Their laughter tickled the breeze. It was a view only money could buy, she noted. Three months? Three months of feeling like the Queen of the Blue Ridge Mountains? She sighed. Of course she could do it! Someone had to do it, she laughed.

Mahalia unpacked her overnight bag, and then stood in front of the mirror. For a few minutes, she brushed her hair, and then tied it back up. No point having it wild and unruly while she cooked. With a little lip balm, she moisturised her lips, and was ready to head off to the kitchen. But the curious side of Mahalia led her further up the hallway, peeking inside each bedroom. Each of the eight rooms—was it eight? She was losing count!—was beautifully decorated, but none, she noticed, had fresh flowers by the bed.

And for a second, just a second, she wondered if Beau Candler had set Keith up to terrorise her so that she'd have no choice but to move in here. Don't be stupid, she snapped at herself.

This must be his room, she smiled, and noticed a banjo on the end of the bed. Who needs two banjos? she wondered, and before she knew it, Mahalia was standing in his room, surveying his sleeping quarters. Not a single thing was out of place. No clothes lying around, no scuffed shoes in the corner. Everything was in order, except the banjo. Beau Candler didn't strike her as a musician, let alone a man who played banjo. The scent of spicy aftershave greeted her, as she peeped into the en suite. And her belly somersaulted at the memory of him standing close to her. It was like he was right there, in the room with her. Quickly, she turned around, startled. Of course he wasn't here. It was just aftershave! The scent of desire taunted her and she felt giddy with anticipation. They'd almost kissed in her grandfather's kitchen. She was sure of it. Surely it would happen here?

The guilt of being in his room, uninvited, had her scooting down the staircase, and back into the safety of the vast kitchen. Once there, she felt calm again, and breathed in the simplicity of the design. Everything, apart from the centre island, was white: pure and clean. She noted the flowers on the black-marble work area: irises. So, he liked flowers too, she thought, and then wondered if perhaps there was a woman around even though she hadn't detected any trace of one.

Mahalia made herself familiar with the layout of the kitchen, and gathered utensils around her. Natural light poured in through the large glass doors and glass ceiling of the conservatory-style kitchen. What a perfect environment to work in, and such a bonus for her photography.

Mahalia searched inside the box of vegetables that she'd brought with her, and began to prepare a Thai meal: jasmine rice, coconut curry, fresh greens with ginger and sesame dressing, and sticky rice with mango.

While she expertly chopped the vegetables, she breathed in the heavenly scent of lemongrass. Within seconds she was singing her favourite song.

As the curry simmered, Mahalia explored the

kitchen some more, and noticed a CD player on top of the double-doored fridge. Inside a basket was an assortment of CDs. She popped it onto the counter, and looked through them, smiling when she realised that every one of them was country music. So, he likes a bit of Bluegrass himself, does he? Something in common, I suppose, she thought to herself. They were all by the same record label: *Candler Ridge Blues*, based in North Carolina. Cassidy Mage was the artist she chose, and immediately hummed to the haunting melodies. After she flipped to the artist biography inside the CD cover, she read about how Cassidy was discovered at the Emerald Tavern. Mahalia had heard of that place. It wasn't too far from her café.

The name of the label seemed familiar, too. In fact, she was sure she had several of their CDs. It was North Carolina based, but she didn't know much more than that. Born and raised in Asheville, she loved the city. It was one of those places that stays in people's minds long after they leave. It featured distinctive restaurants, including her own café, art galleries, locally-owned craft shops, and a rich architectural heritage. People came for art, they came for healing, and they came in celebration of the bohemian way of life.

It was the Appalachian culture which most intrigued Mahalia, but if she was honest, it was easy to take everything about the area for granted. She had no intention of ever leaving Asheville; she loved the mountain city, its eclectic downtown and thriving culinary culture. And then there was the music scene, too, of course, and the beautiful Appalachian mountains. It nestled comfortably between the Blue Ridge Mountains and the Great Smoky Mountains of Western North Carolina. People flocked to the city, for it was a treasure trove for shoppers. It meant that her café was always busy.

Whenever she'd been away, she felt her heart swell with joy upon her return. Just watching the city rise up out of the mountains was like something from another world. Even the climate was welcoming. Mild summers, afternoon thunderstorms just to liven up the air, and a vibrant Fall with beautiful autumnal foliage.

Just as she was about to turn the steamer off, Beau's Jaguar pulled into the driveway. From her vantage point in the kitchen, she watched him step out, and pull his briefcase out from the passenger seat. Beau was dressed in a business suit, and as soon as he walked away from the car he started untangling his tie. She laughed to see how frustrated he was in trying to escape from its noose. Mahalia longed to run her fingers over his chiselled features. *Smouldering, that's what he is.*

'Hey,' he said, carefully placing his brief case on the floor, giving her a broad smile. 'Mahalia, it smells terrific. I sure am hungry. Hope you've made plenty!'

'Should be enough,' she smiled. 'But you'll have to wait a minute I'm afraid. I need to take some photos first.'

The counter, where she'd set up a mock studio, had whole coconuts, and one cut in half. There were sticks of lemongrass and a handful of white rice scattered carelessly across the bench.

Beau hoped that she'd clean everything up before she went to bed that night. There was nothing worse than waking up in the morning to a messy kitchen. And for a split second he wondered if he'd regret having her take over the kitchen. Just for a second. How could he regret having her in his home? In his life? The next three months would be just the balm he needed. Perfect timing, really, he mused.

Mahalia set out the food, and began photographing from various angles.

Beau watched her as she studiously focused on each shot, seeing the setting through different eyes and different lenses. Aware of his stomach growling he said 'I suppose I'm going to spend the next three months eating cold food,' he laughed.

'Hey, it was your idea for me to come here. I said I'd cook,' and she returned his laugh with a giggle, 'I never said anything about the temperature of it!'

Mahalia laid the camera down, and then looked at him squarely in the eye. 'Where do you want to eat?'

Beau was bamboozled by the question, but more than that, it was how he had to catch his breath when she looked him in the eye. It hadn't occurred to him that they might eat anywhere other than the dining room, and then he realised how ridiculous it would be for the two of them to sit at a table for fifty.

'It's a nice evening, we could eat in the garden,' she suggested.

'Or the balcony?'

'Wherever you like,' Mahalia answered, setting the plates onto a tray.

'What do you think of Cassidy Mage?' he asked, curiously.

'Cassidy? Oh, the singer! Love her. She has such a unique tone. I find her quite soulful.'

'Yes, that's what I thought.'

'So, you like Bluegrass too? Locational hazard, I suppose...'

'Occupational hazard, actually.'

'Occupational? What, you mean you *work*?'

'You thought I sat on my backside all day did you?' he grinned, and led her to the balcony as he carried the tray.

'I just figured you didn't need to work.'

'I don't.'

'So, why do you?'

'Because I love what I do…and, even rich people need a reason to get out of bed in the morning,' he laughed. 'Wealth shouldn't make people less passionate about life. Cooking's your passion, right?'

'Yes, it is. I find it contemplative, artistic and the whole process is,' she paused, 'for me, dynamic and inspiring. I discover something new about myself every time I create a recipe. As long as I'm coming from my heart, rather than my head, then the possibilities are endless.'

'My sentiments exactly,' he smiled.

'So what do you do, Beau?'

The sound of her voice, and the way she said his name, did something inexplicable to him. Who'd have thought a one-syllable word could be spoken in such a way as to define him in the manner he'd sought all his life: with respect. 'I have a boutique recording label.'

'Not Candler Ridge Blues by any chance?' she laughed.

'The one and only!' Beau sat the tray down on a wrought-iron table on the balcony, overlooking the back garden. It was parklike, with mature trees, vast swathes of lawn and a lily-covered pond with pergola and decking. 'I look for raw talent. People who haven't been noticed by producers or labels, and I sign them up.'

'Lucky them! Cassidy is a gem. I bet she couldn't believe her luck when you turned up.'

'I don't know if it is luck. People like her have generally done their work. They've sung their way around bars and clubs, and are committed to their music. All I do is sit up and listen.'

They both set out the plates, glasses, napkins and cutlery.

'Mahalia, I'm going to a small venue tomorrow to see a singer who was recommended to me. Would you like to come with me? That is, if you're allowed some time off from your photography?'

'Sounds fun! Are you sure I won't be a nuisance? I'm afraid that I'm a bit of a Bluegrass groupie!'

'One-hundred-percent sure.' Beau realised his life was about to change in ways that he'd never even considered. Was it destiny that brought Mahalia back into his life, or just plain good luck? Whatever it was, he had no intention of letting her leave anytime soon.

Beau savoured every mouthful, enjoying the mingling flavours of fresh ginger root, exotic lemongrass, tangy lime and creamy coconut.

Sunlight glinted against Mahalia's copper ringlets, and it was all he could do not to reach over and run his fingers through her hair. To distract himself from other thoughts, he tried counting the freckles on her face. Try as he might, he couldn't contain his arousal. He was a man, after all! Three months of living with her was going to drive him crazy.

Beau doubted he was going to get through the rest of the evening without carrying her to his bedroom. In his mind, they'd already made love on the kitchen counter, on the staircase, outside her bedroom, in his bedroom.

'What?' he asked, when her question knocked him out of his fantasies.

'How did you get into having your own label?'

'I play a bit of Bluegrass myself, but I figured that with the family name I'd only ever be seen as someone cashing in on my ancestral legacy. In the end, I realised I didn't need an audience. I was quite happy to strum along at home, perhaps write the occasional song, and have someone else record it. What's the point in coming from wealth if I can't help others along the way?'

'Wow, that's… well, rather philanthropic.'

'It's a business, not a charity,' he laughed. 'No one gets a free ride. More wine?' he asked, pouring some into her glass. As he reached his hand out to hers, the electricity between them sparkled. 'Thank you for such a pleasant evening. I can't remember the last time I enjoyed myself so much,' he said.

'So that's where you're hiding,' came a voice from behind Mahalia. Startled, she turned around to see a short woman, wearing a red jumpsuit, and five-inch red heels. Her bleach-blonde hair was worn in a chignon, and diamonds hung from every available part of her body.

'Margaret! What are you doing here?' Beau stood up, his voice a clear barometer of his anger and shock.

'This is my home, too. I am your wife, after all. I have every right to be here,' she said, looking pointedly at Mahalia. 'Entertaining, are we?' Sarcasm twisted into sweetness like molasses on sand, impossible to separate the two.

Mahalia disliked her immediately, and not because she was Beau's wife. As an excellent judge of character, everything about this woman rang alarm bells. But damn it, why didn't Beau mention that he was married? And more importantly, why hadn't her grandfather ever told her? He knew how much Mahalia fancied Beau. After all, it was he who had nursed her through the drama of teenage love-sickness for goodness sake!

'You don't live here, and the sooner you sign those damn divorce papers, the sooner you won't be my wife!'

'I'll just leave you two alone,' Mahalia said softly, making her way to the door.

'You're not going anywhere,' Beau said firmly. 'You're my guest, and the only one leaving is Margaret.'

The blonde woman reached forward to shake hands. 'Margaret Pilkington-Candler, pleased to meet you. As you've heard, I'm Beau's *wife*,' she said, emphasising the last word in such a way as to make sure Mahalia would never, ever forget who she was.

'Mahalia Mason. Really, I'll just leave you to it.' No sooner had the words left her mouth, than she felt Beau's hand on her arm calmly restraining her.

'Please stay. I'm sorry she ruined our lovely evening, but I can assure you that she's not staying here.'

Like a mouse pulled between two ferocious cats, the last place Mahalia wanted to be was between a warring husband and wife.

'Margaret, this house isn't part of your settlement. Right now, you're trespassing.'

'Oh Beau, don't be so possessive. I've told your lawyers,' she purred, 'I want half of everything. Almost eight years of marriage must account for something? And until everything is settled, I can live in any one of *our* houses. And right now, Red Maple Manor is where I want to be.' The woman's satisfied grin had Mahalia wanting to scratch her eyes out. It wasn't jealousy, but fury at the level of manipulation this woman exercised.

Beau growled, and then said 'Tonight only. One night, and then you're gone. I mean it, Margaret.'

The devious smile on her lips made Mahalia sick to the stomach. Why would he ever have married someone like her? It didn't make sense. Opposites might attract, she told herself, but they're more likely to repel. To her mind, their coupling was utterly repulsive. Beau Candler was a good man and deserved better than to be with someone like Margaret.

Walking back to the table, Mahalia packed their plates and glasses onto the tray, and quietly found her way back to the kitchen.

Margaret sauntered up the hall, smug, satisfied and scheming.

'I am so sorry. I had no idea that she'd turn up here. She hasn't been to this house in years. She doesn't 'do' the countryside. Margaret lives in Boston and New York, and rarely goes anywhere that doesn't have bitumen.'

'Look, large as this house is, and as kind as your offer for me to stay is, this clearly isn't going to work. The place isn't big enough for two women, Beau. And...' It was now or never. She had to say it: 'I really like you, but whatever I might be feeling, and forgive me for being so bold, I think you feel the same, this is way too messy and complicated. I'm going to go back to granddad's house, and I will bolt the door. Don't worry. I'll be safe.'

'No.'

'Beau, you can't stop me,' she said with determination as his hands came down gently on either side of her.

'One crazy woman on my hands is more than enough. I don't need two of them. If you're going back there, then I'm coming with you. Don't argue with me Mahalia. Please. I'm not in the mood.'

Beau placed his fingertips deep into his closed eye sockets, hoping that it might take away the first signs of a tension headache.

'I'm okay, really. It's best if you sort things out with your wife,' Mahalia said kindly.

'She's not my wife! Well, she might be on paper, but that's all it ever was.'

Mahalia sensed his desperation.

'Let me grab a few things, and I'll meet you in the car.'

'If you insist,' she sighed. Mahalia realised there was no point arguing. There was no way that Beau was going to let her stay at the homestead alone, not while Keith McVeigh was alive. Mahalia cleaned up the kitchen, and then grabbed her toiletry bag from the ensuite. There was no point packing up her bag, as most of her clothes were back at the house. Decidedly uncomfortable about the glamorous Mrs Pilkington-Candler being in residence, she prayed that she'd be gone by morning. That wasn't the only request she sent, prayer-like, up to the heavens.

A Dream Come True

They sat on the verandah of Mahalia's new wooden house—the old homestead was little more than a shack, really, and far from new—and sipped crisp white wine until the stars winked that it was past their bedtime. For Mahalia, it was a dream come true. Perhaps she should be thanking Mrs Pilkington-Candler!

'How did you and Margaret end up together?' she asked casually, realising it was a rather loaded question. 'I just don't understand it. You're such an odd pairing.' Perhaps she was being too forthright, but his relationship with Margaret really bothered Mahalia, not just for her own selfish reasons, but because he deserved better than that. Finally, she understood the source of the sadness she'd detected behind his eyes.

'We met properly the same year that I met you, actually. The big difference was that she was my age, and you were a schoolgirl.'

'I'd have waited,' she smiled, teasing him with her long lashes. 'I really would have!' Although she laughed, there was a depth of seriousness pushing those words forward.

Beau wanted to run his fingers down her dimples and trace the way they etched into her cheeks, and then kiss her forehead. Mahalia was a gorgeous woman, and yet he could see the lovesick teenager speaking up and having her say, and he found it rather endearing. He wanted to hug both the girl and the woman.

'So would I,' he sighed. 'So would I. God, I wish I had!' Beau was silent for a long while, gathering his thoughts. 'Margaret's family had long been connected with mine, mostly through our fathers, but I wasn't remotely interested, however the pressure from both families soon built to the point where it seemed marriage was unavoidable and inescapable. I hadn't even asked her to marry me, yet both of our mothers were booking wedding venues, dresses, photographers. The whole nightmare just exploded in front of me.'

Mahalia looked at him, and said 'You just don't strike me as a man who can be told what to do. I don't get it. Why marry someone you're not in love with?'

'I wish I could answer that. I really do. I suppose I looked around me and saw that I'd not had any successful relationships, and that perhaps the idea of waiting till "the right one comes along" was just a myth. I was twenty-five years old. There were expectations around me.' Beau sighed at the realisation that his life could have been so different, if only he'd spoken up instead of being railroaded. 'The night before we got married, I had a nightmare. I was walking into a long black tunnel. There was no light at the end. If only I'd known how prophetic it would turn out to be.'

'Do you still think that's true: that myth of the "right one" coming along?'

'No. I believe that there's a true love for everyone, but one thing's for sure: I won't be getting married again. Ever! Thank God we didn't have children. No man needs a rope around his neck,' he said, hitting the seat beside him, a small testament to eight years of anger and frustration.

Mahalia felt herself wince as if his words were a personal attack; and after waiting a few moments, stood up, collected the wine glasses and headed into the kitchen. And finally, after all these years, she put any fantasy of being with Beau to rest.

'I'll just make up the spare bed,' she said, walking down the hallway. Beau was right at her side.

'There's no need for that, Mahalia. No need to create more washing. I'll just share your sheets,' he smiled, his hands reaching around her waist.

Beau was surprised when she didn't respond in the way he hoped; in the way he *expected*. Beau was convinced that the attraction was mutual. What the hell had changed?

When she turned around, and looked at him, he was consumed by her vibrant smoky-green eyes.

'Beau, I don't do one-night stands, and I don't do flings. I'm an all or nothing kind of girl, and you're clearly not an 'all' kind of boy...*man*. I'll make the spare bed.'

Without saying a word, his lips said more than he ever could. The sounds coming from the depths of her told him quite clearly that making up the spare bed was not going to happen. They'd find a compromise.

'Not here,' she whispered between breaths. 'Not in the hallway. Come...come to bed.'

'Are you sure?' he groaned, desperately hoping she'd say yes.

'Yes.'

Beau lifted her up into his arms, and carried her down the hall through the opened door. The light from the hallway cast itself dimly into her sleeping space.

The room smelled of rose incense, and he could see that although the rest of the house was filled with unopened boxes, she had unpacked the bedroom.

A lovers' nest, he thought to himself. Perfect. But he couldn't help wonder if she'd been expecting company. Gently, he placed her onto the rose-pink patchwork quilt on top of the bed. It was piled high with cushions in every shade of pink. Beau suddenly found himself believing in fairytales. He had thought of Mahalia, and her long copper hair and glistening green eyes, so often over the years. In his mind, they'd made love up on the mountain trail, their horses tied to the trees, more than a thousand times. But now, here they were, and it was really happening. When his hands touched her smooth face, it was a promise that he would go kindly to her remote locations. A promise, that no matter what, she was *not* a one-night stand. Beau wanted to tell her that he'd waited for this night for a long time, but somehow when it came to forming the words they felt trite. Corny wasn't going to do. Perhaps it was better not to say anything at all. Instead, he let his hands do the talking, and his lips, and his tongue. With each touch, he gently undid the life she knew. Whatever failed dreams they'd had, or sacrifices they'd made, seemed irrelevant now. They were together, at last.

'What are we going to do about contraception?' he asked softly, tenderly stroking her hair.

She sat bolt upright. The truth was she hadn't thought of something so...so *mundane*! Mahalia's breathing was rapid.

'I...I hadn't thought,' she said, feeling foolish.

Beau reached his arms around her and laughed gently. 'Well, I guess we're just going to have to wait then, aren't we?' he smiled.

'That sounds like torture. You have no idea what my body feels like right now.'

'I think I have a pretty good idea!' he laughed, rolling her onto her back, and kissing her bare belly. His arousal showed no signs of abating. He knew exactly how her body was feeling.

Mahalia's hips rose to meet him, and he slowly made his way further down. 'There's nothing to say I can't leave you sated, and looking forward to the next time,' he teased. If only they'd have stayed at his house; he'd at least have had condoms nearby. Though they were probably well beyond their expiry date! But this wasn't the moment for cursing. Beau was grateful that he was here.

Beau thought about her as the seventeen-year-old girl he'd met up there on the mountain, and the woman she was today, here in his arms. And then he wondered how many lovers she'd had.

They lay in each other's arms for some time, long after they should have been asleep.

Mahalia ventured into unsafe territory, because curiosity got the better of her, and she just had to ask: 'Tell me about you and Margaret.'

Beau let out a long groan; he didn't want that woman in bed with them!

'Even though it was quite clear that we weren't well matched, and I most certainly didn't want to spend another day with her, there is a sense of failure associated with divorce, and that doesn't bring me pleasure. That she left me for her personal trainer is pretty indicative of the lack of attention I gave her. I was relieved, but ashamed that I hadn't been a good husband. I hadn't been a husband at all. I can't say it didn't affect me. But, I've hit rock bottom. That's where I am now. Right now.'

'Hitting rock bottom is a good thing, Beau. It's a solid foundation, and you can rebuild your life from here.'

As Beau held Mahalia close, he luxuriated in the feel of her against his skin. Beau had waited years for this moment, always dismissing his daydreams as an impossibility.

'I want her out of my life. She can have everything I own, if that makes her happy. But I suspect that even that wouldn't be enough. And if she senses I've moved on—and no doubt seeing you in the house will add fuel to the fire—then she'll hang on just to spite me. I can promise you, though, there is nothing there between us. There never was.'

Mahalia sighed. She certainly didn't want to see the woman again, but the truth was that she wasn't entirely happy staying here with Keith McVeigh just up the road. Perhaps she should just return to Asheville and make the most of trying to photograph her book from the busy hum of the café.

'Tell me about the men in your life,' he asked calmly, not really wanting to hear the truth about her lovers, but feeling that it was important to know her past.

'Nothing to tell you, Beau. I've dated some men, quite a few actually. About twenty, in fact,' she confided, surprised by the look of shock on his face. 'Nice dinners out, walks up the mountains, visits to art galleries, but nothing serious. No rabid men are going to turn up at my door, if that's what you're expecting. There was a man once, but...' and she giggled. 'I was jailbait, apparently.' She tickled him and Beau quickly brought himself on top of her, promising, *promising*, but not going any further. Not yet. Not tonight.

'There must have been someone serious. You said you don't do one-night stands, so...there must have been men you've slept with. What's wrong? What did I say? I'm sorry, it's personal. I shouldn't have.'

'I haven't slept with anyone before.'

'You mean?'

'Yes, that's exactly what I mean!'

'But, you looked like you knew exactly what you were doing. I had no idea.'

'I was only responding to what you were doing to me! How could I react any other way?'

'God,' he whispered, breathing into her long hair. 'I wish I'd known.'

'What would you have done differently?'

'Everything. Absolutely everything. I promise that next time we're in bed together, that I'll....'

'Don't promise me anything Beau. Just kiss me!' Of one thing she was clear: Mahalia didn't want him to do anything differently!

Ghost

Mahalia and Beau breathed a sigh of relief when they arrived back at Red Maple Manor to see that Margaret's car had gone. After the night they'd shared, they simply wanted to spend the day together without interruptions.

On the kitchen counter, Margaret left a long letter with unreasonable demands on property settlement. Beau was furious.

'She can have the lot!' he snapped. He just wanted her out of his life. And why now? Why was she back now when he hadn't heard from her in months? The timing couldn't have been worse. Beau wouldn't put it past her to cause merry hell between him and Mahalia. Margaret was manipulative, conniving and controlling. If only he'd recognised that in the first place, he'd never have married.

Mahalia spent the day pottering around the kitchen, taking longs walks, and shooting photos of her food creations, and of the garden, and more than a dozen photos of Beau. Her favourite was the one of him in his recording studio, headphones on, tapping to the beat of a new song he was listening to. In that moment, he had no idea that the lens was focused on him, anymore than he did after they'd walked, hand in hand, up to the little church house and she'd photographed him lying in the long grass and wildflowers by some weathered tombstones. When she photographed their lunch, he had no idea that she wasn't just taking pictures of the food and décor, but of him savouring every mouthful.

Beau proved to be a wonderful subject: radiant like the first light of sunrise, his smile warming her heart; the way his strong jawline gave her a sense of solidity, and how he walked with the ease and grace of a lion, his muscles lean and taut.

If every day was like this, the next three months was going to be one rather erotic and pleasurable dream. For both of them.

Beau loved having her padding around barefoot in his house, singing to the great singers of Bluegrass, such as Alison Krauss; and filling the space with her joy and effervescence. Beau helped her wash up the dishes from their evening meal, and then, checking his watch said, 'We'll need to leave in about half an hour if we're going to get to the Emerald Tavern. Is that enough time for you to get ready?'

Margaret had always insisted that she needed three hours minimum to prepare herself for any evening out, but he could tell that Mahalia was not high maintenance in any shape or form.

'Sure, I'll be ready.' She flashed him a smile which captured just how wonderful the day had been. Mahalia was floating. They both were. They'd found each other, and it was as if a long-held dream had come true.

When she headed to her ensuite, it felt like the height of luxury to stand in a marble-surround shower which had views over the hills. Three months? No, she could have a whole lifetime of this, thank you very much!

Taking her cue from the venue, she wore a simple emerald dress which suited the Spring evening perfectly. It hugged her ample breasts, and came in tightly at the waist, only to fall away loosely at the hips and drape around her in swathes right down to her ankles. Then she slipped on matching sandals, and wore her long hair loose. It was a dress she'd worn dozens of times, but when Beau saw her walk down the staircase she suddenly felt like it was worth a million dollars. That *she* was worth a million dollars.

'Wow.' He didn't know what else to say. 'Wow.' He'd only ever seen her in jeans before, but watching her move so elegantly beneath the sheer fabric, he told her that she was born to wear dresses. Dresses like this one. 'You look beautiful.'

They drove to the tavern, and conversation was easy. Laughter came naturally. Mahalia found his humour to be a delight.

Beau parked the car in the safety of a hotel car park, paying the valet to look after it while they were out.

The music exceeded both of their expectations, and although the singers Beau chose for his label were few and far between, he was almost certain that he'd take two new singers from tonight.

Russ Thesan, a young Australian singer finding his feet in the mountains of North Carolina, had a rare sound that made Beau sit up and listen. The young man wrote all of his own material, and that was always a bonus. His falsetto was breathtaking, and Beau noticed the goose bumps on Mahalia's arms. 'You can't let him walk away,' she whispered to Beau.

'I have no intention of letting him go anywhere but to my recording studio,' Beau promised, squeezing her hand just that bit tighter. He loved that they were on the same page, musically.

Lola Honey was a sweet young Irish singer on her first trip to the USA, making her debut at The Emerald. Beau wanted to sign her up without question; and in a fatherly way, felt a tad possessive. She was young, but so brilliant.

Mahalia found Lola's passion contagious; it seemed only natural that she'd ended up living in the Appalachian Mountains.

Lola told her: 'Bluegrass is such a cool sub-genre of country music. Did you know that it has its roots in Welsh, Irish, Scottish and English music? And when you mix that with a little African-American jazz, you've got Bluegrass!' Mahalia didn't have the heart to tell her that she knew everything there was to know about Bluegrass. Lola sipped on her wine, and explained how the immigrants from Ireland and Great Britain arrived in Appalachia in the 18th century, bringing their musical traditions with them: Scottish ballads, Irish reels, accompanied by a fiddle. Lola was determined to follow in the footsteps of her ancestors, she said.

Beau took their contact details, and arranged for Russ and Lola to come by his studio at Red Maple Manor, and to talk deals.

Mahalia admired Beau as he worked: he was so casual and friendly, yet intensely passionate, and always professional.

They spent the rest of the evening tapping their toes, unable to keep the smiles off their faces, or their hands off each other. Near the end of the evening, they were on their feet slow dancing. It was a perfect night, and one Mahalia hoped she'd never forget. She was falling for Beau Candler, and there was nothing to catch her.

It was well past two in the morning when they arrived home, exhausted but happy.

'Your bed or mine?' he asked as they walked up the staircase.

'Ours,' she said, leading him into the guest room. 'Ours.'

They were too tired to make love, which surprised both of them, but they knew they had time. All the time in the world. Drifting off into deep slumber, and listening to each other breathe, brought a soft comfort to them, while their naked bodies wrapped around the other. Pleasure, protection, safety.

The sounds of fiddle, mandolin and banjo accompanied their delicate and fragile dreams.

Mahalia felt so happy. This was like a dream come true. Beau was humorous, kind, attentive: a gentleman. And it seemed that he genuinely cared about her, and showed it in his every action. When she was with him, she felt different. And she had never felt like this with any man before.

How did this happen so easily? That was the last thought Mahalia had as she finally went unconscious to the hoot of an owl, and the scent of mountain air. They fell asleep, hand in hand, smiles on their faces.

They'd been asleep for about an hour, when something— she wasn't sure what—pulled Mahalia out of her deep sleep. Groggily, she turned her head and looked up to see a figure standing in the room, hovering just above them. Barely able to make out the face in the pale moonlight, Mahalia's screams made Beau sit up.

'What are you doing in here?' Mahalia yelled, pulling the sheets up to her shoulders, and covering her naked breasts.

'Margaret, get the hell out! Have you no respect?' Beau was out of the bed, not giving a damn that he was buck naked. 'Get out!'

Pointing towards the doorway, he yelled again. 'Now!'

Margaret walked out slowly, aware that damage had been done. She was pleased, very pleased, that the full impact would be felt for a long time to come. Even in the dim light, she made sure that Mahalia could see the smile stretched out across her face, and knew that Beau would follow her out.

Mahalia's breathing was rapid. The fear, coursing through her veins, made her feel as if her life was in danger. She didn't know how to calm herself down. What was Margaret doing here in the middle of the night? In their bedroom? How long had she been standing there? What was she going to do? Mahalia had never felt so terrified in her life. Margaret made Keith seem like a teddy bear. Was this how her relationship with Beau was going to be? Would she live in fear of Margaret turning up and spreading her poison whenever she felt like it?

Although she already cared deeply for Beau, she didn't have the strength to live with this gravity always hanging over them. Something had to be done, and it had to be done now before things got even more out of hand. The woman was evil. Mahalia wrapped a robe around herself, and headed down the stairs to the join them. They were nowhere to be found.

When Mahalia walked into the kitchen, just before turning the light on, she noticed their silhouettes outside near the fountain, the moonlight reflecting their animated conversation. It was pretty obvious from Beau's hand actions that he was not happy. Not happy at all.

She was in two minds about whether to join Beau, and beat the woman over the head with a broom, or to stay inside and be patient.

First light was stretching itself across the new day, and they were still out there. Mahalia was desperate for sleep. They'd been out there for hours. Finally, she had enough. That woman had to go! If Beau wasn't going to move her along, then she had no choice but to take action herself.

Mahalia made coffee for two, and took the cups outside as she walked barefoot across the dew-covered lawn and passed one to Beau. She felt Margaret look her up and down, distastefully.

'About time this little show was over, isn't it?' Mahalia said firmly, staring into Margaret's eyes in a way which made it clear just who was living in this house now. She was not giving up what was hers! Margaret may have Beau's name, but that was all. Mahalia had his heart. She was sure of that.

'Come inside Beau.' But she didn't plead or beg or whine. It was a simple statement, and without a backward glance, walked inside, holding his hand. Beau was right beside her without question.

That simple gesture told Margaret that she had a lot of work to do. *Fight fire with fire*, she thought, looking at Mahalia's red hair glinting in the early light. She slipped into her BMW and screeched down the drive, flicking white pebbles up like ocean waves. She was not done with Beau Candler, and she'd wipe that contented look off Mahalia Mason's face if it was the last thing she ever did!

Coffee was sipped quietly in the kitchen, and then Beau walked Mahalia back to bed. Their bed.

'I wish I had an excuse for her, but I don't.' Beau turned on the bedside radio, and Alison Krauss and Vince Gill came on singing *I've Been Trying to Get Over You*. He flicked the station, and Clare Bowen and Sam Palladio sang *When the Right One Comes Along*. 'That's more appropriate,' he smiled.

They slipped beneath the covers, and found solace in each other's arms. Beau so desperately wanted to make love to her. It would have been easy. His aroused body made it quite clear that he was ready. But not now, not after the devastation that Margaret had left in her wake. The timing was all wrong. They'd wait until their hearts were pounding with ecstasy rather than fear. And if Beau was honest, he was scared. Bloody scared! He was scared he'd never be rid of Margaret, and he sensed Mahalia was scared of the very same thing.

Gravity

The next week passed in a contented haze of fabulous never-ending food, affectionate embraces, long kisses, bursts of laughter, and walks through the woods and up the mountain. Mahalia continued photographing everything that caught her eye, including the debonair man with the tempting smile.

Beau headed into town to pick up supplies for Mahalia, and threw in a few packets of condoms. *Tonight.* Yes, tonight they'd finally make love. Enough time had passed since Margaret's horror visit. Life felt calm and peaceful again.

When he arrived home, Beau found her barefoot in the kitchen, singing. It was his favourite image of her, and he'd grown to treasure it so quickly. Beau realised he couldn't imagine a time in his life where she wouldn't be there. It shocked him to his core. Damn it! He *needed* her. When the hell did that happen? How did it happen? But he knew that was a silly question. It happened because she was so easy to be with, and because she had a good heart. There was no hidden agenda, no deviousness. With Mahalia, what you saw was what you got. And from her, Beau got a whole lot of laughter, enthusiasm, thoughtfulness, and inspiration. She was a woman who lived her dreams, and believed in herself. Mahalia had no need to make anyone do anything they didn't want to do. Finally this was a new chapter in Beau's life, and he found himself praying that they'd walk through the following chapters together, stepping into Happily Ever After. More than once he was astonished at how quickly his views on life and love and commitment had changed. But could someone as self-sufficient, confident and carefree as

Mahalia Mason ever need a man like Beau Candler? A man who had married in haste, and not for love? A man who preferred his own company to that of other human beings? A man who had spent years enjoying living on his own?

Mahalia licked the avocado off her fingers. If only she'd known how seductive he found it, and how such a simple action taunted him.

'Hey, try this,' she said, inviting him to sample the artichoke and tomato bisque.

Taking a more civilised approach, he dipped a teaspoon in. His mother would have scowled at the finger dipping.

'Mmm. Good. Excellent. When can we eat?'

'Soon,' she smiled. And he knew what "soon" meant: after three hundred photos from every possible angle! Beau listened to the sound of his tummy rumbling. Food had never been much of a diversion for him before, until Mahalia walked into his life, into his kitchen...and back into his heart! With growing impatience and hunger, he watched as she arranged the blueberry and pinenut quinoa salad, and then the parmesan pumpkin dumplings.

While she was getting everything just right, he walked to the other side of the kitchen and helped himself to the minted-chocolate mousse. Well why not? It had his name written all over it, or so he told himself.

'I've got eyes in the back of my head, you know,' she laughed, and came rushing over with a wooden spoon to tap him on the knuckles.

And then she had a better idea, and used her camera as a weapon instead, taking just the perfect shot of his chocolate-covered fingers as they hid the treasure in his mouth.

'Here,' she said, passing him a table cloth and some cutlery. 'Go and set us a space down by the oak trees. Let's eat out there tonight. It's such a beautiful evening. I'll bring the rest out.'

Mahalia followed him out across the lawn, and they picnicked under the crimson setting Sun and canopy of red maple leaves.

'I could get used to this,' he said, hoping she'd understand the full meaning of his words. When he realised that she'd been deeply hurt by his comments, that night on the homestead verandah, about never wanting to be married again, he wondered if perhaps he'd spoken too quickly. And then he mentally chastened himself. 'Don't be a fool! You hardly know her.'

They talked about Lola Honey, and how he'd already arranged some tour locations with her in mind. There was no question that he'd sign her up, and when she'd come over the day before to do a recording, they were both so pleased with the arrangement.

For quite some time they lay on the grass, holding hands, and kissing each other gently. It was time. Time to take her inside and make love. Slowly. Beau wanted to devour her in a way that they'd never forget!

'I'll wash the dishes,' he said, 'and I'll meet you upstairs.'

Beau found it rather charming that she should blush, and turned away so that she couldn't see he was smiling.

Mahalia didn't go upstairs, but hung out in the kitchen with him while he packed up the dishwasher. Then, Mahalia walked up behind him, and put her arms around his waist. Just those few kisses on his neck, and he knew he wasn't going to make it to the bedroom.

Damn. He felt like an impulsive teenager, not a grown man.

Tring! Tring, tring! Tring!

'Who the hell is phoning at this time of night?' he wondered, thinking it was perhaps one of his overseas talent. 'I'm sorry,' he said, the pain of separation on his face saying far more than his words ever could. Reluctantly, he pulled himself away from the treats on offer. So close, but yet so far. He should have let the answering machine kick in.

'Hello?' he answered gruffly, his mood changing at lightning speed from the amorous, lust-filled emotions of a moment ago.

'Yes, it is. No. Yes, I am, but...'

There was a long silence. Beau hit the kitchen counter with his fist.

'Yes, I'll be there.' He slammed the phone down, and thumped the wall.

That ashen look was about to tear them apart.

'Beau?' Mahalia was too scared to ask what had caused him to be so angry, but what choice did she have?

Beau wrapped his arms around Mahalia, and held her tightly. He didn't know how to say it, or indeed how she'd react. This was the last thing they needed, and the timing was lousy. Beau kissed her gently on the forehead. This was an altogether different kiss from less than a minute ago. This wasn't a kiss inviting her to untold pleasures. No, this kiss was saying: *Sorry. Forgive me for what I'm about to do. Wait for me.*

'Margaret's been in a car accident,' he groaned. 'She's on life support. It's touch and go.' He ran his fingers through his dark hair in exasperation. 'The hospital hasn't been able to track down her parents...

They're abroad, and out of reach. I'm...'

'You're next of kin?' she sighed.

Nodding, he affirmed that, of course, he was next of kin.

Mahalia wanted to thump the damn counter too. That bloody woman! Mahalia was fuming inside, but outwardly she remained calm. The last thing Beau needed at a time like this was her having a meltdown.

Mahalia couldn't help but ask 'Was it an accident?'

'You think she did this on purpose? It's possible. Nothing she did would surprise me. I need to fly to Boston. Now. God, I'm so sorry Mahalia.' He shook his head in disbelief.

'There's nothing for you to apologise for.'

Beau was touched by how supportive she was, but then again, he wouldn't have expected any less of her. That was why he'd fallen in love with Mahalia. What? Could it be true? Was he in love? Already? But now didn't seem the right time to tell her. He wanted to do it while they made love, cocooned from the world.

'Is there anything I can do to help you pack? Do you know how long you'll be gone for?'

'I have no idea. I'll call you when I get there and have spoken to the doctors. I've got a house in Boston, though I'm not likely to stay there as it's Margaret's main residence. I'll probably just stay in a hotel. I'll be back as soon as I possibly can. I promise.'

Beau packed in haste, gave her a long, tender, meaningful kiss, and then reluctantly drove to the airport.

Mahalia let the tears slip from her eyes. It wasn't that she didn't feel sorry for Margaret—she wouldn't wish that on anyone—but why couldn't that woman just stay out of their lives? Why couldn't she just move on? Wasn't it obvious to Margaret that she and Beau had nothing, nothing whatsoever, in common?

Mahalia headed up to Beau's bedroom, and turned on the Jacuzzi in his ensuite. If he couldn't be here with her, then she'd at least stay in his bedroom and absorb him in that way. Slowly, she eased her body into the warm bubbly water, and let her tension melt away. It would have been so much nicer if he was here with her, but she'd make the best of the situation and look forward to his return. Beau might not have plans on getting married again, and she could live with that: but she sure as heck couldn't live without him. Mahalia convinced herself that marriage was nothing more than a piece of paper, and what did it mean for Beau and Margaret? Nothing. Well, nothing but trouble! No, what Mahalia and Beau had was real. No legal document in the world could match their...what was the word she was looking for? Oh. Yes. That was it: *love*. Nothing could match their love. In that moment of realisation, she sank beneath the water and symbolically let herself drown. When she emerged, her copper ringlets wet and defined, she sighed deeply: *I'm in love with Beau Candler.* And then she laughed out loud. *I fell in love with him eight years ago. This is nothing new!*

Beau phoned as soon as he consulted with the doctors.

'Her chances of survival aren't good,' he said slowly, his voice tired and weary.

'I'm so sorry,' Mahalia replied, and Beau was

deeply moved by her sincerity. Despite the chaos Margaret had whipped up into their lives, Mahalia genuinely cared for Margaret's wellbeing and recovery.

'I'm heading off to the hotel now…this is the number, and my room number. Call me if you need anything. Anything at all.'

'I will. Try and get some sleep, Beau. It's pretty exhausting doing full-time hospital visits,' she said, remembering her grandfather's last weeks on Earth.

'I'll call you in the morning, honey. Good night.'

'Bye.'

Mahalia missed having Beau to cook for, and had to remind herself with each meal that she was now cooking for one. Just one. Not two. No duet, no doubles. No tango.

Single. Solo. She hated it!

She was confused. Mahalia had always thrived in her own company, and loved being alone for long swathes of time. Why did it feel so torturous all of a sudden? How was it that she could barely get through the day now that he wasn't at her side? It was utterly ridiculous. Mahalia was a successful, confident business woman, used to taking care of herself, her café and her life. Where was all this neediness coming from?

Beau had been gone for two weeks, now, and still there was no improvement.

'They've asked me to consider turning off her life support. I don't want to make that decision,' he said, the full weight of it hitting his voice with gravity unlike anything he'd ever known. 'This shouldn't be my job. I don't have any emotional connection to her. I never

51

have. I have to decide in the next couple of days.'

'Would you like me to come over?' Mahalia asked.

Beau was taken aback by her concern.

'That's really kind, but no. I want to keep you separate from her, as much as is possible, that is. I'll call you tonight,' he said.

Mahalia had planned on cooking some Indian food for the foreign section of her book, but decided it was far too beautiful a day to be trapped indoors. Instead, she took a drive down to Asheville, checked in on her café, and caught up with the news. The staff members were handling things well. It gave her great comfort to know they could be relied on, and that she didn't have to worry.

After a cappuccino, she headed down the street and sought out a selection of eclectic, handmade photo frames from local craftspeople. Mahalia wanted to surprise Beau when he returned, and have some of her favourite photos of him on display around the house.

The ringing phone startled Mahalia from the depths of a spicy dream. It was 3am.

'Honey? I'm so sorry to get you out of bed, but Margaret is awake!'

Mahalia rubbed her eyes and suppressed a yawn. Was this real or part of her dream?

'She's awake? Wow. That's....that's great news Beau.'

'I can't tell you what a huge relief it is. I had agreed to turning off her life support after the priest had been in. There appears to be no permanent brain damage. I haven't seen her yet. I'll go in first thing in the morning, and then see what I can do to get her parents back in the country. She'll need a lot of care.'

'She's very lucky to have you, Beau.'

There was something about those words—words said with care, love and kindness—that made him feel uncomfortable. Margaret doesn't have me, he said to himself. She's never had me. And he felt like he had something crawling all over his skin. It was irritating. And he would do whatever he could to eradicate it—her—from his life. For a moment, he wished Margaret had...and he chased the thought away.

Beau arrived at the intensive-care ward at 8am. Margaret was drowsy, but aware. Nurses hovered around her, checking vital signs, writing down notes. The smell of starched uniforms and the bright fluorescent lights were far removed from the creature comforts he'd been enjoying with Mahalia.

'My darling Beau,' Margaret said, her words slow and careful. 'You're here.'

And in that gut-sickening moment, he knew that the car crash had been no accident. She probably hadn't counted on the fact that it would nearly kill her, but she had relied on her husband to be at her side. Damn her! Damn Margaret Pilkington! Beau felt his body fill with hate, and was about to walk out when the doctor came through, smiling with relief at Margaret's progress.

'All the tests show that there's no permanent damage. It's miraculous really. We'd like to keep her in for a few more days, but then she'll need full-time care for a few weeks or so until we're happy that she's back to normal.'

Beau's heart fell to the floor. 'A few weeks?' he asked incredulously. Where the hell were her parents?

He was fuming. The conniving, manipulative bitch! She had planned this well, knowing her parents would be out of reach.

As soon as the doctor left the room, Beau said 'I'll hire a live-in nurse, but if you think for one second that I'm spending any time with you, you can think again. You are not my wife. You never have been!'

Beau left the private room, and headed down to the cafeteria unable to get his head around how a person could be so calculating. What did she want from him? Why would any sane woman want to be with a man who didn't like her; didn't love her? No, he thought to himself, she's not sane at all.

Beau brought his laptop into the ward, and carried on with work. There were emails to reply to, recordings to listen to, and concert-tour dates to confirm. Not for a minute did he pay any attention to Margaret, but no one could accuse him of not being by her side in her hour of need. There in body, but not in mind or heart. Margaret would never take those from him.

By day, he craved the evenings when he could phone Mahalia for hours, and listen to her lyrical voice. He longed to hear about what meals she'd been making, or where she'd walked to.

Beau found himself living a whole lifetime in their conversations. They were becoming closer all the time, despite the miles between them. In some ways, the separation was good. They were able to discover more about each other without being sidetracked by the physical temptation of each other's body.

Talking on the phone allowed them to listen, really listen, to what the other was saying. They cherished these moments of each day, even the comfortable silences in their conversations. It was like a homecoming.

'I'm sorry Mr Candler, but we can't discharge her without your signature assuring us that you'll be with her night and day for the next few weeks.' The doctor looked at him with a heavy sense of responsibility, urging Beau to take the pen and sign his life away.

'Why can't I hire a nurse? Surely she'd have far more skill than me in detecting if anything is amiss?'

'That's true, but what she needs right now is emotional support, and that isn't something you can buy.'

Beau glared at the doctor, and caught the smile on Margaret's face. Oh yes, she had Beau just where she wanted him. But not for long. Not if he had anything to do with it.

Beau begrudgingly pushed her wheelchair down the corridor, and hissed 'Don't expect anything from me!'

When Beau and Margaret arrived at their Boston home, the maids were scurrying around getting everything in order. It made him realise how glad he was to be living in the mountains, in his own space. What a charade, he thought.

True to character, Margaret called on Beau for her every whim.

'This is why we have maids, Margaret. Ring the bell for them, not me! I'm not here to cater to your needs.'

'But I need you for my emotional well-being, honey. That's what the doctor said, remember?'

'Don't ...*don't* call me honey! Don't call me anything!'

Dutifully, he checked on her several times each day, but said little. Beau employed two full-time nurses, and kept maids on around the clock.

Sure, he had to stay in the house with her, but he didn't have to endure her company.

'Lola, that's fantastic! Brilliant news,' Beau said down his cellphone, turning his back on Margaret at breakfast the next morning. 'Let me just check the dates,' he said, looking through his diary. Damn. If he wanted to see Lola perform at Nashville's iconic Bluebird Café it would mean that he'd have to go straight there from Boston, which meant it wouldn't give him a chance to see Mahalia. He was torn. Beau's heart said there was only one choice, but his sense of responsibility as an agent and promoter told him otherwise.

It would only be an extra three days away, and they'd been apart so long already. Surely it would be okay? Their relationship was intact, and blossoming beautifully. They could endure this.

'Yes, I'll meet you there. See you on Friday. I'll be at the Hilton Hotel. Can't wait. And hey, well done!'

The next call he needed to make was to Mahalia. Beau left the room so Margaret couldn't hear the conversation. Somehow he expected resistance from Mahalia; he expected a fight...but what he got was the woman he loved, encouraging him and Lola. Beau pinched himself, and more than once reminded himself that Mahalia wasn't Margaret. Sure, she had a temper when she needed one—he witnessed that the day Keith McVeigh had her baled up in the barn—but she wasn't controlling or manipulative. She didn't have a deceptive or nasty bone in her body. It was strangely refreshing, though disconcerting after so many years with a woman like Margaret pulling the strings.

'I can't wait to see you,' she whispered down the phone. 'Can you take some time off when you get back? I'll need to start again at the café next month, part-time at least, and…and it would be really great if we could spend some time alone, just the two of us, before I do. And Beau, I want you to make love to me. I don't want to wait too much longer!'

'Me either! The diary is clear. It only has your name in it,' he promised, and they could both feel the depth of that promise crackling down the phone. By closing their eyes, they could feel the other's hands on their skin, the scent of their hair, the warmth of their breath.

Beau was going to have to talk to her about going back to work at the café though. Really, how was that going to work? She couldn't commute for two hours every day. They'd have to work something else out.

Tomorrow he was flying to Nashville to watch Lola perform. Tonight was his last night in Boston, and he needed to finalise things with Margaret. That she was so accommodating, caught him off guard. His gut told him not to trust her.

'Yes, I'm happy to just have the Boston house and one of the New York penthouses. I'm sure I'll manage with those, and with the villa in Barbados for retreat. I guess I'll get by.'

Ungrateful cow, he thought. Margaret had brought nothing to the marriage, and was walking away with six million dollars in property, and a decent cash settlement.

'I guess I'll get by?' he repeated sarcastically.

Beau caught his breath, and forced himself to calm down.

'The solicitor is here. Please sign the damn divorce papers.'

'Yes dear, whatever you want. Have a good time in Nashville. And…enjoy your life.'

Beau hoped, he prayed, that it was the last time he'd ever have to set eyes on Margaret Pilkington again realising that he didn't have a single positive memory about her. Not one.

Lola's debut at The Bluebird Café was well received, and Beau was grateful that he'd made the decision to travel to Nashville. It was a highlight for any country-music artist to sing to the small intimate crowd at this venue. Afterwards, Beau went through the tour plans he had for her, and talked about getting an album out for Christmas. It would mean a lot of work and time in the studio. They chatted late into the night, and the following day he showed her some other well-known venues in Nashville, and took her to his favourite recording studios. Beau introduced her to many people who'd be invaluable to her career. Lola was a treasure, and he wanted to make sure that she always had the best of everything. Talent like her simply didn't come along every day. Beau was thankful for the time they spent together, and getting to know more about her personal life. Lola had recently lost her brother, and taking the plunge into her singing career had been deeply therapeutic. Beau had suspected there'd been trauma, as it weaved its way into many of her song lyrics. *Heart-wrenchingly beautiful*, was how Mahalia described them.

In a couple of days he'd be flying back to North Carolina, and he couldn't wait. He'd spent far too long away from Mahalia. They had lost ground to make up for, and more than anything he just wanted her in his arms. Needed her in his arms. More than anything, he wanted to tell Mahalia that he loved her.

Laced with Poison

Mahalia was frying some pakoras, and setting the stage for an Indian photographic shoot, laying out all sorts of colorful spices on the bench, when she saw a black BMW ease into the driveway.

'Oh no,' she groaned as soon as she realised who it was.

What the hell does she want now? I thought she'd signed everything? Mahalia's mind was racing. She felt distinctively uncomfortable with Beau's ex-wife—soon-to-be ex-wife—turning up while he was down the other end of the country. Beau told her that the solicitor made a house call to Margaret to ensure that everything was signed, and that their divorce would be finalised soon. Why was she here? What did she want from Beau now?

Mahalia's heart raced like a fever through her body. Her thoughts were chaotic.

Should she be gracious? Should she demand that Margaret go away? Mahalia was at a loss to know how to deal with the situation. And then she reminded herself that the woman, no matter how much she despised her, nearly lost her life. This was no time to be mean. If she'd travelled all the way from Boston, then she must have had a good reason. The gentle side of Mahalia brought some calm to the situation, but she was determined not to be taken advantage of.

'Margaret, what can I do for you?' Mahalia asked coolly as she opened the front door.

'May I come in?'

'Beau's not here. I don't see why...'

'I know. He's in Nashville. I thought you and I could have a little...chat. You know, woman to woman? Wouldn't that be nice?'

Mahalia couldn't think of anything worse, and she most certainly didn't want that woman crossing the threshold!

'What is that divine smell?' she asked, pushing her way past Mahalia. 'Beau said you were putting together a little book of recipes...' and she followed her surgeon-sculpted nose all the way to the kitchen. The same kitchen she could never be bothered to cook in because it was too far away from the night lights of Boston and New York. Margaret may not have had time for kitchen knives, but her whole body was a testament to her love-hate relationship with surgeons' scalpels.

'I don't imagine he said "little" book,' Mahalia replied.

'Well, you know what I mean!' and she laughed it off in that dismissive way she had about her.

Mahalia wished she could insert poison into one of the cookies that she was offering. In her mind, she already had Margaret dead and buried under an oak tree. She could do it, she told herself. The adrenalin rush would give her the strength to drag her out there and to dig a deep hole.

'What do you want to talk about?' she asked, bringing herself to the real world.

'You and Beau...whatever it is you think you've got? It's over. You've had your fun, and now it's time to leave.'

'I beg your pardon?' She was incredulous. Margaret may have been a number of years older than her, but there was no need to treat her like a girl!

'It's time for you to leave, Ms Mason. I'm Mrs Candler. And I'm the only woman Beau will ever be married to. I'll make sure of that. You know, he was so caring and kind while we were in Boston together.

It reminded him of the olden days, and ...well, it's time for you to leave, dear. Beau loves me. He's never stopped loving me.'

Mahalia thought of the pitchfork in her grandfather's barn. That would be more efficient than poison. Yes, she could see it now: bury the fork and the nightmare of a woman together. Margaret wasn't the sort of person that people would miss.

'I'm carrying his baby...' and she let the words sit in the kitchen, like baking soda and vinegar frothing up.

Margaret picked up the cookie, avoiding eye contact, and said 'These aren't too bad, really.' Turning the cookie over and studying both sides of it, she finally took a bite.

'What? He hasn't had sex with you!' Mahalia yelled, furious at the woman's blatant lie.

'He didn't tell you?' Margaret's voice was cool and calm. 'I guess he didn't want to hurt your feelings. He does have a soft spot for you, I suppose.' The saccharine-coated words seeped down into Mahalia's soul, invading her inner peace like dye being dispersed into her veins and pushing its way up to her heart. All the way to her heart. 'I'm sure you think you're in love with him dear,' her words were carefully crafted, cruel and suffocating. 'But, oh, how can I say it? You were nothing more than his little plaything. I'm the woman he's going to be with now. We're having a baby. So, pack up your things, dear, and get on with your life somewhere else.'

'Who the hell do you think you are? You get out of here!'

'Would you like to see the pregnancy test? Would you like the doctor to confirm it for you? Perhaps a copy of the DNA test would satisfy you? I can prove it, you know.'

Jesus! Sweet Jesus! The woman was either a real nutcase or…she was serious.

Could it be true? Surely not? Beau had spoken to her every day on the phone, sometimes four times a day. Not once had she detected any change in his affection or devotion to her; and he promised he was coming back soon.

Margaret stood up, surveyed the kitchen and smiled. 'It will be so good to be back here, children running around on the lawn.'

Mahalia showed her to the front door, and said 'Don't return. Never come back!'

Mrs Pilkington-Candler left quietly, and drove away with a saccharine smiled pasted to her face.

Mahalia raced to the toilet, and was sick. All evening she tried phoning Beau, but his phone was out of range. Damn! Of course it wasn't true, but a little voice inside her head kept eating away at her and destroying the faith she had in him. She had to be honest with herself: the truth was that she didn't know Beau very well. Fancying a man was one thing, but truly *knowing* him? That took a lifetime.

By midnight, she'd packed her bags and boxes, and in the morning she called a delivery company to take them back to Asheville. In such a short time, she'd come to love Beau more than life itself, she couldn't deny it, but if Margaret *was* carrying his baby—and she must be, if she offered to show proof—then there was no place for Mahalia in his life. It was time to move on, and forget he ever existed.

Mahalia cried more that night than she had in her whole life. Letting go of Beau felt like an impossible task.

The publishing deal was secure, and it wouldn't be too hard to stage photo shoots from the café—she'd probably have to do it in the evenings—and she could even do some from her apartment.

Living in Beau's house had been a dream, and everything about their relationship was easy: except for the dealings with his wife. It wasn't fair! But what choice did she have?

Moving On

The first thing Mahalia Mason did when she moved back to her Asheville apartment was to change her cellphone number. It had to be a clean break, no matter how soul destroying it was. No matter how much she missed Beau, she had no choice but to cut him out of her life. With Margaret's baby on the way, that woman would be indelibly entwined in his life forevermore. No, she had no choice but to move on. Heartbreak was tormenting her, night and day, and threatened to bring an end to all the hard work she'd done on the book. Mahalia wanted to throw away everything good in her life and run away; far, far away.

After a long conversation with her sister, Anita, she even thought of joining her in Australia. That way, there was no chance she'd ever run into Beau again. It would truly be a fresh start. Anita told her to stay where she was; that her life was in North Carolina, and that things would resolve with Beau. 'Hang tight, Hali,' she said more than once.

Fortunately, Mahalia's dedicated café team were thrilled to have her back, and their warm welcome was just what she needed to help her find the strength to take one step at a time. She was grateful that they were all so reliable and efficient, and took pride in their work. Mahalia had to admit that she rather enjoyed being back in the hum of café life, and the thrill she got when seeing people walk by the front windows; and how they were magnetically drawn in by the aromas, the sounds, and the laughter. The way their eyes lit up when they stepped inside and were consumed by the ambience: immediate devotees to the magic and inspiration Mahalia had created there.

Today Beau would arrive back at Red Maple Manor, and notice that she was gone. It was possible that he'd come looking for her at the café, but as she was spending most of her time away taking photos, the chances were good that they wouldn't see each other. Most of the time she managed to focus on her work, but no matter how hard she tried, Beau's face, his hands, his voice and mannerisms, seemed always to be on the periphery of her every waking thought and sleeping dream. With every tick of the clock, he was there, right beside her. And yet, when they were together, she had no sense of time. She couldn't even remember the clock ticking. Mahalia fought to escape his memories, but the task seemed insurmountable.

Beau's face lit up into a huge smile as he circled in front of Red Maple Manor. It felt so good to be home again. But more than anything, he wanted to wrap his arms around Mahalia. The past few days had filled him with frustration. He'd not been able to get through on her cellphone. Strangely, it kept saying 'out of service', and the home phone rang out. Despite being apart from her in recent weeks, he was used to hearing her voice sometimes four times a day. The past three days had been intolerable. Beau found it hard to function without her laughter and conversation as an anchor in his life.

No matter, in less than a minute they'd be in each other's arms again: where they both belonged.

'I'm home!' he yelled, wondering why he couldn't smell anything cooking in the kitchen. Odd, he thought. He was used to being greeted by cinnamon, ginger, chocolate, limes, garlic, and other sensuous treats. Perhaps she's taking a nap, he thought, knowing how fond she was of leisurely rests whenever the mood struck. All the horses were in the front field, so he knew she wasn't out riding. It was the maid's day off, so he couldn't ask her about Mahalia.

He ran up the staircase, two steps at a time. Disappointingly, she wasn't in her room, or his room. He checked all the other bedrooms, just in case. And then Beau went back into her room. Disbelief gripped him in the gut. Shock left his mouth dry. Beau's suspicions were confirmed when he opened the wardrobe to see it empty. Completely empty.

'What the hell?' he yelled, raking his fingers through his hair.

Beau ran back down to the kitchen, and pulled open the pantry and cupboards. All her kitchen items were gone. He was going crazy. Why? *Why?*

It didn't make sense!

Beau headed into the lounge room, and several large photos caught his eye. This is new, he thought to himself. Eye-catching portraits of Beau gathered themselves along the top of the mantelpiece. And in that moment, he realised that he'd never seen himself that way before: happy.

Unsure which was his favourite: lying amongst the wildflowers at the church house; smiling in the studio with headphones on; or being caught with his fingers in chocolate pudding. Maybe it was the one with his bare feet in the cold water of the stream, sunlight in his hair, fir trees behind him?

The room seemed so different: alive, personal, real. It felt like...*home*. She had done this. His beautiful Mahalia. The wild gypsy with the long copper hair had made his house a home. Despite his wealth, he'd never been able to achieve what she managed to with a small selection of photographs. But where the hell was she?

Beau looked in the garage. There was no sign of her pick-up truck.

And then his heart somersaulted. No. Surely not? He couldn't bear the thought of her being at the old house with Keith McVeigh on the loose. He scrambled into his Jaguar, and raced down the road, defying every rock and stone and pothole. To hell with it, she needed him!

When he arrived, Beau was taken aback by the local realtor, Bob Basiner, hammering a *For Sale* sign into the ground.

'What the hell are you doing, Bob?' he demanded, after winding down the car window.

Catching Beau's fury, the balding man replied defensively: 'Ms Mason has it on the market. Quick sale, is what she said. Just following instructions.'

'Take the damn sign down. She's not selling, and if she insists on it, then rest assured I'm the only person who is going to buy it!'

Beau moved past Bob, and grabbed the key from under the mat on the verandah. He couldn't believe it when he walked inside. *Empty.* Completely empty. Beau went to the bedroom. *Gone.* Not a trace of her here, apart from the faintest hint of rose incense and a bare mattress. Damn it! Where was she?

A nervous sweat was building up as he headed outside again. He hated this. He hated not knowing where she was; not understanding why she'd leave without a word. Without goodbye. His mind raced through all their recent conversations. There was nothing, nothing at all, that he could pinpoint to her change of heart.

'Bob, I said take the damn sign down! I've bought it. I'm buying it. I'll come to your office right now and buy the place. Just get me the god-damn forms and I'll sign them.'

The man scuttled back to his car, packing the wooden sign into the boot.

'I'll see you there in ten minutes.'

Beau read through the paperwork far quicker than he'd ever read through any legal document in his life.

'Has she accepted my offer?' he asked abruptly.

'She wants to know who's buying it. She says she won't accept anything until she knows who it is going to.'

'It's nothing more than a rundown shack on ten acres of land. Why's she being so stubborn?'

'Do you mind if I ask why you're so determined to buy it?' the man asked.

'Because I don't want her to regret selling it. And she sure as hell will.'

'Isn't that her right though? To regret it?'

'Just find a way for me to sign those papers. I'm not leaving until I do. Five times the market price. Offer that to her.'

The man was flustered, and went into another office to make the call.

'Ms Mason the gentleman is offering you five times the market price. Offers like this don't come along every day. I urge you to take it. In this economical climate, it's not even worth the asking price, Ms Mason. Will you accept his offer?'

'What's his name?'

Bob didn't answer.

After a moment of silence, she said 'It's not Beau Candler, is it? Tell me it's not Beau.'

'I'm afraid it is, Miss. Will you accept his offer?

Now it was her turn for silence. For a few fleeting seconds, she thought of what she could do with all that money. A holiday would be a good start! Some remote island to escape from Margaret Pilkington and the baby!

'Tell him,' she took a deep breath, hoping she wouldn't regret the words about to escape her lips—the same lips he'd kissed so many times—'Tell him that I will only sell at market value.'

'Yes, ma'am.'

Bob took her condition back to the table.

'Is she crazy?' Beau asked.

'It would seem you know her better than me, sir,' Bob answered tactfully.

'Sold!'

Beau walked out of the office, stunned. Why didn't she take the money? He returned inside and asked to look at the documents again, and quickly scribbled down her address. Mahalia wasn't getting away from him that quickly!

Beau had never driven down the mountain to Asheville so quickly in his life. Even though he was aware of breaking every speed limit, he didn't care. This was urgent. Exhausted after travelling all night, he wasn't going to let that get in the way. Some things in life just couldn't wait.

The first stop was her café. Idling at red traffic lights, he felt his impatience exploding. Looking at the map, he figured he had about two blocks to go before he reached Citrus Avenue Café.

Beau was shocked at the lengths she'd gone to cut him out of his life. Why? Everything was so...*perfect*. They had so much in common, they were attracted to each other; their conversation and laughter were easy. What was the problem?

But the question he should have asked was: *who* was the problem?

When he finally pulled up out front, he couldn't help but smile. It was like looking at Mahalia: beautiful, refined, full of flavour, a hint of wildness and a sense of the exotic. It left him curious, wanting more. Wanting to taste, to consume. It left him taunted by desires that he didn't know were possible. Like a magnet, he was drawn in. Powerless. God he missed her!

The pavement was lined with more than a dozen lemon and lime trees in large, cone-shaped, silver stainless-steel pots. The outdoor tables were made of wood, and padded orange cushions lined every chair. Bunting, sewn from orange and lime fabric triangles, hung across the front of the verandah like a garland, and Bluegrass music played through speakers, inviting customers to sit around for one more song, one more coffee...oh, and yes, one more slice of lime and coconut cake. Beau filled the parking meter with coins, then headed inside the café. It was breathtakingly beautiful. He'd never been in a place quite like it: elegant, sophisticated, and yet casual and inviting.

'May I help you sir?' a pleasant young woman asked him.

'I'm looking for Mahalia,' he said.

'She left five minutes ago. She's gone for the day. Can I leave a message for you?'

'No, that'll be fine thanks. Perhaps I'll have an Americano, with hot milk. Thanks.'

'Coming right up,' and when she smiled at him, Beau knew exactly why Mahalia had hired her. The young woman had the same sincerity that she possessed. This is what she wanted her customers to feel: that they were valued. No wonder she was such a successful business woman; she put her customers first.

Beau made himself comfortable at a corner table, and closed his eyes to listen to the music. The singer was Jamie Bradner, the second talent that Beau had signed to his label. The irony of hearing Jamie in Mahalia's café didn't escape him.

Just one coffee, and then he'd drive to her house. Just one coffee. He planned the conversation they'd have, and he'd get to the bottom of her hasty retreat. One thing was clear: he wouldn't leave Asheville without her.

Beau made it back to the car just as the parking attendant was deciding to hang about and give him a ticket.

'Not your lucky day, mate,' Beau laughed, getting behind the wheel just in time. And he hoped it was going to be *his* lucky day. He estimated that he'd be at Mahalia's within ten minutes.

Good taste, he thought to himself as he wheeled into the tree-lined street. It was a fairly modern apartment building, and he could tell which was hers from the balcony alone: it was a riot of flowers, with tubs of plants from one end to the other, mostly filled with herbs. If only he'd known that it was a clue to where she was right now.

Beau felt nervous as he approached the door, and reached up to knock.

No answer. He knocked again. Where the hell was she? He cursed under his breath, and went back to the car to wait.

It was only midday, but he'd already had such a long day. He'd taken a late-night flight from Nashville back to North Carolina, and should have gone straight to bed. That had been his original plan. That is, until he arrived home to find Mahalia gone. Then everything changed.

May was Mahalia's favourite time of the year, and she always marked it on her calendar as sacrosanct: The Asheville Herb Festival. She arrived filled with joy, and tried to let go of the fact that she'd just sold her dear grandfather's sweet little homestead and land to Beau Candler, and by default to Margaret Pilkington-Candler. She wasn't going to think about them right now. No siree.

Mahalia wandered through the stalls, taking time to immerse herself in all the offerings: herbs, handmade plant-based soaps, books, vinegars, crafts, medicinal herbs, culinary herbs, gifts, lotions, teas, dried flowers, tinctures. Oh yes, she was in herbal heaven. It was a paradise for herb lovers, and right up her organic street. Amongst her purchases was balm, and she considered it a metaphor for the healing which needed to take place. It wasn't long before her basket was overflowing with goodies; some for the café, but mostly for her own pleasure. Mahalia mingled amongst the other 25,000 herb lovers, in the Mecca of plants.

As she saw familiar faces at her favourite stalls, she smiled, and more than once laughed that it was like a family reunion. For half an hour, she chatted with Jacquie at the Appalachia School of Holistic Herbalism, and then moved on to the Bee Log Farm, convincing herself that a few bees on the balcony would be good for the street. The basil nursery had her sighing with joy, and in that moment she was back in time eating a tomato and basil sandwich with Beau on his balcony. Time to move on, she told herself as she breathed in the scents of the Blue Ridge Soap Shed stall. It was hard though. *How do you ever let go of someone who has touched your soul?*

'This is one of my favourite stalls,' she said affectionately as she handed over money for a year's worth of soap.

'And you're one of our favourite customers,' Mary Ellis laughed. 'Did you win the lottery?'

'Feels like it,' she smiled, aware of the cost involved in selling off her land and feeling a tad guilty for spending money before it had arrived.

And how could she walk past Mudluscious Pottery and Gardens without buying several of their hand-thrown pots?

'Can you deliver again to me this year?' she pleaded.

'Yes, Ms Mason,' Henry Brass said. 'We'd be happy to. Though if I remember from last year, there's not much room left on your balcony!'

They both laughed at the truth of that.

Red Moon Herbs was her next temptation. Well, she told herself, I need something to put in all those pots! Mindful that she was going overboard, she reminded herself that a little retail therapy was just what she needed right now; something to numb the dull ache inside. Oh how she missed Beau! What she'd do to wrap her arms around him, just one more time. But she couldn't. Not now. Not now that he was going to become a father! The thought of him making love with that evil woman made her want to scream. Hadn't their time together meant anything? She genuinely thought he cared for her! Maybe he'd got fed up of not

'We haven't had sex for eight years…since… our wedding night. Once, only once.' Beau stopped laughing, and his face took on a serious expression. 'I couldn't keep having sex with her when in my mind I was making love to you! I had enough respect for the three of us to know it was never going to happen again. I've been nothing more than her trophy husband. Nothing more than someone who could keep her in the style and luxury she covets so badly. I was simply someone who enabled her to keep having her photo in the society pages. She knew from day one that my heart wasn't with her; that I'd fallen for the redhead on the mountain.'

Beau walked closer to Mahalia, desperate to put his arms around her, but she backed away. Unsure. Still so unsure. There was something about her that reminded him of a nervous filly. He had to earn her trust again. He backed away to give her some space. Beau had time; and he'd take all the time in the world, if that's what it took, to win her back again. With horses, you waited until they came to you… Beau knew that he just needed to stay within close range, and that she'd soon start to feel safe. It wouldn't be long now, and his arms would be around her. Not long. One step at a time. Slowly. Slowly.

'Honey,' he said, seriously. 'She's playing you.'

'She's not pregnant?' Mahalia asked in disbelief.

'Not to me!'

'Oh.' She took the words in slowly. 'But she said she had proof.'

This time, when he moved forward, she didn't back away, but instead, moved into him. It had been too long. Within seconds they were back in each other's arms, where they belonged.

having sex with Mahalia, and succumbed to the normal hormonal needs of a man. Maybe Margaret was just in the right place at the right time? Damn it, she thought, it should have been me!

Mahalia's legs felt like lead, now, and she moved on slowly. Settling herself on a chair in the Somewhere in Thyme Herb Gardens stall, she closed her eyes and breathed in the delicious scent.

By the time she left the festival, her pick-up truck was heaving. *All in a day's work*, she told herself. *Don't feel guilty for buying a few herbs*. But her little shopping spree had set her back about three weeks' pay. She wondered if she'd have gone so overboard if Beau hadn't bought her house and land. Just knowing there'd be a lump sum coming in gave her free rein to max out her credit card. Thanks Beau, she laughed into the afternoon breeze.

It was early evening when Mahalia's pick-up truck pulled into the street.

Beau recognised it straight away. Where had she been all this time?

Beau stepped out of the car, and met her at the side of her truck.

'What's going on honey? Why have you left me?' he asked, his eyes looking as bruised as he felt. 'You *have* left me, haven't you?' he asked, but he knew the truth of the matter.

'It's obvious are lives are going in different directions.' She looked at the keys in her lap. Mahalia couldn't bear looking into his eyes. Beau looked so hurt, so unsure of himself. That wasn't the man she'd grown to love. No, not at all. That man was strong, confident, capable.

'I thought we were doing well. I thought we were happy. Mahalia, *look at me*. Please.' That was more like it; more like the man she knew. He was firm now, intolerant of the situation. 'What's going on?'

Mahalia pushed the door open forcing him to move out of the way. 'You better come in for a minute,' she said, carrying as much as she could of the herbs. Beau followed her cue, and carried several bags.

'Got enough herbs here?' he laughed, trying to lighten the mood. 'Not the best time to sell your land if you've got nowhere to plant these?'

'I've got the balcony,' she said firmly.

Beau looked around her apartment as she led the way across the open-planned living area towards the balcony. Mahalia opened the glass sliding doors, and placed the bags and box of herbs down. Beau followed her back into the kitchen. It was painted in sunflower yellow, modern, and well lit. Not surprisingly, there were a few vases of spring flowers to brighten the place up. It made him smile to think how she always beautified her living environment with flowers.

'Mahalia, look at me please. Stop avoiding my eyes.'

Slowly, she looked up.

'I know Margaret's accident wasn't helpful to our blossoming relationship,' he said. 'The timing was lousy! It was a long time for you and I to be apart, and I'm sorry that I went straight from Boston to Nashville. I really am. But she's signed the papers and accepted my offer. I'm free of her. We're free of her.'

Mahalia could see a sense of jubilation in his tired eyes. But what about the baby, she wanted to know. Didn't he see that as a hindrance to everything?

When she didn't reply, Beau said 'The photo
fantastic! I can't believe how much life they bring t
house. I just need you back there. It's so empty wi
you. Please, come back. What can I do to bring
back? Just tell me. I'll do anything!'

Was he pleading?

'And what about the baby?' she demanded
had to know.

'Baby?' Beau looked utterly confused. 'V
baby? Are you… *pregnant?*'

She thought for a second that there was a tw
in his eyes. 'How could I be pregnant, Beau? We ha
had sex! *Margaret's* baby.'

'Margaret's having a baby?' he asked. 'I d
know she was seeing anyone at the moment.
what's her baby got to do with me?'

'Your wife came to visit me with her joyous n
that she's carrying *your* baby. Why the hell do you t
I left?'

Beau laughed. He laughed out loud. He lau
so hard he had tears coming out of his eyes. Then h
on the nearest chair while he composed himself.

'It's no laughing matter, Beau! How could
do that to me? To us? I…I thought we had somet
special!'

'Do you *really* believe that? You really believe
I'm the father?'

'Of course! Women don't lie about such thing

'Women like Margaret do! If it's my baby, ther
the longest pregnancy in history!'

'What do you mean?' And what's so darn fun

Mahalia's hands were firmly on her hips.
eyebrows were knitted tightly in fury.

'Don't ever walk away again,' he whispered into her ringlets of fire. 'I couldn't bear it. Promise me that you won't leave?'

'I can't make a promise like that,' and she pulled her head away from his shoulders and looked into his eyes.

'Why?' he asked, desperately searching for answers.

'Why? You tell me that you can't promise marriage to a woman, but you ask me to not leave you. It doesn't work like that. The first night we spent together you were adamant that marriage was a noose!'

And this time she did pull away. Mahalia headed to the kettle, then filled it up, and turned it on at the wall. Placing two cups on the bench, heating milk on the stove, she finally looked at him again. It was the longest minute of his life. Beau broke the silence, unsure of the best way to say what had to be said.

'I don't want to be apart from you, Mahalia, but...I can't put myself in a position of feeling trapped again, like I did with Margaret.'

He hoped she'd understand. It was all so simple in his mind.

'Trapped?' she asked incredulously. 'Don't you know me at all? I'm nothing like Margaret!' She was furious. How could he even compare them? 'I don't want a trophy husband. I make my own money; I have my own business—a thriving one, actually—and my own home. It might not be a manor or a penthouse, but it's home. *My* home. And I love it. I don't need anything else! I don't need a man to buy me things! I can't believe you'd even compare me to her...to that...woman!'

'I know you're nothing like her...' Beau felt ashamed that it had come across that way. 'I'm sorry.

What I meant was that I...' He shook his head. 'I don't know what I meant. There is no comparison.'

'Have your coffee, and then leave. You want freedom, and I was stupid enough to see picket fences and children and vegetable gardens with you. They're incompatible desires. Let's just end this now.'

'Mahalia? How can you say that?' This time he was going to be firm. 'No, I'm not walking away from here, damn it! This is exactly what Margaret wanted to happen. We shouldn't be fighting! I don't want marriage, because I don't want a woman threatening me every other day. I don't want a woman standing in the kitchen holding a knife to my throat when I say I've had enough. I don't want a woman who makes me feel useless as a man!'

He could see the expression on her face change. She was trying to read him. What was he talking about?

'Beau?'

'Margaret has always been somewhat unstable. I wanted to end the marriage as soon as it began...but... Never mind.'

'Well I do mind! And I deserve to know what the hell has happened that makes you so unable to say that you'll spend the rest of your life with me! Because, damn it, I know you want to. I see it in your eyes. I feel it in your heart. I sense it when you touch me,' she said the last words softly, and then remembered how angry she was with him. Hopping mad, in fact. But she also felt something growing inside her: *tenderness*. What had that woman done to him? Mahalia moved closer now, and held her hand on his.

'I'm sorry. I don't mean to yell. I want to know what's happened. I want to understand. No matter what happens when you leave here today, I want to understand *you.*'

She thought she saw a tear well in his eye, but it disappeared as quickly as it emerged, and instead, he swooped down to her lips, taking her in his arms.

There was a time for talking, and there was a time for making love. Beau didn't want to talk just now, and he didn't want to think. And he most certainly didn't want to think or talk about Margaret.

'Where's your bedroom?' he asked, his voice gruff, urgent. 'The time for talking is later.'

'First door on the left,' and she was not going to argue. Mahalia had waited too long for this moment. Far too long. It was now or never. They both knew that.

He eased open the bedroom door with his foot, never letting her lips stray from his; breathing her in, feeling her close.

Entering Mahalia's bedroom was like stepping through a portal into another world. It was decorated in lime green, and had a sofa which matched the colour of the bedding and curtains. The floorboards were bare and unpolished, and had large green rugs dotted upon them. He smiled to see a guitar in the corner. She'd never once mentioned that she played an instrument. And Beau realised, in that moment, that he had so very much to learn about her. But it was okay; they had a whole lifetime to learn about each other. He'd make sure of that, with or without a damn marriage certificate!

There was no resistance. Mahalia was ready. By the time Beau had stripped off her lilac-coloured T-shirt and ankle-length floral skirt, he was beyond tormented. He laughed a little to see that her underwear matched the colour of her bedroom.

'You take colour co-ordination to a whole new level, Miss Mason,' he smiled.

Oh how she loved the sound of his baritone voice, and that his two-day stubble slightly grazed her cheeks. And the way he nuzzled at her neck, leaving kisses right down to her breasts.

Any sense of head ruling the heart flew out beyond her lime-green curtains and down onto the tree-lined street below. There was nothing here but *heart*. Two hearts, beating wildly…Two hearts, beating as one.

With soft touch, he held her as if she was the world's most treasured possession, and to him, she was. His hands paused for a moment. For eight years he'd wanted to make love to her; eight years of torment of being tied to the wrong woman, and eight years of desiring someone he thought he could never have. Sure, he'd been with other women along the way, but never for long. The guilt of adultery made sure of that!

'Are you sure you want to be with me?' Mahalia asked when his touch slowed right down. She wondered if perhaps he was changing his mind.

'More than anything in the world,' he whispered. 'I just want to savour you; to enjoy every second. I want to remember this for the rest of my life. And I want you to remember it, too. I want you to remember that the first time I truly made love to you was the best night of your life.'

Mahalia kissed him, and it was the most exquisite experience either of them had ever had. They'd kissed before, plenty of times, but this was different. They lingered slowly, their mouths promising things that words never could. Intimacy called them closer to each other's hearts. Couldn't they just stay here, at the crossroads, for the rest of their lives? There was a depth, an intimacy, which etched its way deep into their hearts, and they both knew, without saying, that no matter what, it was their destiny to spend the rest of their lives together. Mahalia had never allowed herself to be this close to any man before, but she wasn't scared. This was sacred ground, and she was ready. Beau was already living inside her heart.

When Beau's kisses invited her beyond the crossroads, they both knew which direction they wanted to go, and with skilled hands he led her forward, tempting her, beckoning her, luring her towards the riches.

Mahalia moved effortlessly beneath him, and as he held himself over her, wanting, waiting, wishing, he knew it was time. There was no holding back, as they gave themselves fully to the other. Every inch of her body tingled with expectation, exhilaration, and exquisite agony. This was the dance of lovers. Mahalia had never felt so happy in all her life.

'Dreams really do come true' she whispered to him. Mahalia moaned, her eyelids heavy as the intoxicating pleasure surged through her.

'You like that, do you?' he smiled, looking up into her slumberous eyes and seeing her drugged state, and feeling rather pleased with his prowess. 'What about when I...'

'I meant *us*, honey. It's a dream come true. I can't tell you of all the nights I cried myself to sleep as a teenager thinking that I'd met the love of my life, but that I'd end up being alone or having to make do with someone else. I didn't want to live a compromised life. And here you are. Pinch me. Tell me it's true.'

She sighed when he changed positions, but he didn't pinch her, he... 'Oh yes, I like that too.' Mahalia couldn't speak after that, but from the deepest place within her, sounds formed and left her body, flying free into the air.

Exploring each other, they marvelled at the pleasures of bodily contact and how good the other felt. Together, they called out into the evening air: it was the call of lovers. The sound of triumph, and surrender. Together, they were transformed. If he died in her arms, right here, right now, he'd have been a happy man. Beau breathed in the scent of the wild-rose oil that she'd dabbed on her neck. She smelled so good, he could barely breathe. Wild rose and sweet arousal. Beau fell asleep counting her heartbeats, and Mahalia fell asleep saying *thank you* to whoever was listening out there in the ethers.

Beau was right about one thing: they'd never forget this night. And through the years ahead, he knew they would often look back, each in their own way, to the night they crossed over. The night they truly became one.

They slept soundly until first light, wrapped in each other's arms. Mahalia's body was still zinging with pleasure.

'Again?' she asked cheekily. 'Do that thing where you...'

'My pleasure,' Beau laughed, and within seconds he was inside her: full, hard, reaching into her deepest desires.

'Oh,' she moaned. 'Oh. Yes. Never stop...'

They slept till lunchtime, and then showered. This was new for Mahalia. She'd never shared a shower before now. I guess it saves water, she thought to herself as she passed the jasmine-scented soap to him.

Beau chuckled at the boxes of hand-made soap

she'd bought from the Herb Festival. 'How much soap does one woman need?' he asked. She merely raised her eyebrows and shook her head at such a silly question.

Mahalia loved how Beau held her from behind, his hands cupping her supple breasts as he nibbled at her smooth shoulders. Slowly, she turned around.

'Are you ready?' he asked, when she looked tormented.

'Hell yeah! What are you waiting for?'

Hot steamy water showered the lovers' bodies. And this was how they spent the next week of their lives. Consumed, consuming. Climaxing. Consummated.

Beau knew that nothing—nothing at all, not even the manipulative Margaret Pilkington-Candler— could get between them now. No, nothing at all. They were rock solid. He was sure of it.

It was a Sunday afternoon, and they'd just come back from visiting an art gallery when Beau decided it was time to tell Mahalia just why he felt so duty-bound to Margaret.

Mahalia listened quietly, not interrupting at all, even when she wanted to scream.

'I think she saw it in my eyes the day she walked up the aisle. That night, after the wedding, she said they looked blank. That there was nothing in them. I guess she was pretty astute. I'd awoken that morning paralysed with fear. I really can't explain why I went ahead with the wedding. Perhaps I was scared of hurting her feelings. All I could think about was you, and why the hell you weren't a couple of years older. Looking back, it would have been nothing at all to wait for, but back then, it felt like a lifetime. I always knew that you were going to get your grandfather's homestead. He used to tell me that all the time. "One day, Mahalia will live here, son." I guess he could tell what I was thinking.'

Beau gulped down the lump in his throat. 'The day I told him I was marrying Margaret, he didn't say a word. He just walked away into his barn putting his hand up as if to say no. I'll never forget it. I don't know if I've ever let anyone down in my life so badly since that day, perhaps apart from myself.'

'Beau,' she whispered, her hand on his.

'You had only just turned eighteen! I was twenty six years old. Everything about it seemed wrong, but obviously the view from where I am now is very different!'

Beau kissed her forehead. If only he could rewind, and start again. He would have waited. Oh God he would have waited.

Beau ran his fingers through her hair, playing with the ringlets.

'I've spent eight years living at rock bottom wondering if I'd ever get out of the hole I landed in. Sure, my business is successful, and I love what I do...but, it has been utter hell being married to her. We may have only been married on paper, but she did everything she could to engineer a lifestyle of greed.'

'Why did you stay married to her? I mean, if it was so obvious from the start why continue?'

Beau stood up, sighed heavily, and walked to the balcony. He smiled as he looked at all the plants there. Mahalia's jungle, he'd nicknamed it. His heart was touched that she was such a nurturing soul, always trying to grow something or feed someone. She couldn't have been more different from Margaret if she'd tried.

Margaret was all about self, and Mahalia was all about helping other people.

Beau found it difficult to say the next words. 'On our wedding night, we...I had sex with her. It could never be called making love because there was no love there at all. It was mechanical.' Beau felt like he was hurting Mahalia by describing this to her, but he knew it was important to share. 'Don't get me wrong, I didn't rape her. I wasn't mean or unkind and I most certainly didn't take her against her will, but I felt as if I was doing something so terribly wrong by having her in my arms when I wanted another woman. When I wanted *you*. Please don't be angry when I say this, but,' he visibly cringed, but Beau knew he had to be honest. 'I wasn't remotely aroused by her, and the only way I could get turned on was by closing my eyes and... pretending I was with you.'

'Beau,' she gasped, a small smile setting on her cheeks. 'Just so long you never think of her when you're with me, then I'll forgive you.'

He felt a surge of relief. 'And the second I thought of you, then the whole thing was over. One picture of your face, your copper hair, your hips, your long legs, your laughter, and I was gone. I'm ashamed to say that Margaret thought it was her who made me come so easily. But it wasn't. I've been haunted by that night ever since, in more ways that one.'

Mahalia wrapped her arms around him. 'I'm glad you thought of me. I'm not glad that you married her, or that you spent so much of your life with her, being married to her, but I'm glad you thought of me, and look at where we are now. Isn't that all that matters?'

Beau held her in his arms, relief washing over both of them.

'There's more. I confessed to her the next day. I had no choice.'

'You told her you were thinking of me? Crap! No wonder she wants me gone. I'm surprised she hasn't tried to kill me!'

'I know.' Beau shook his head. 'I told her that I wanted out. That I couldn't stay married. That I'd made the biggest mistake of my life, and that she deserved the freedom to be with someone who could truly love her. But she didn't want to hear a word of it. We were living in New York, and she broke every item in our house that could possibly be broken. I expected her to be angry, but she was a crazy woman. I left her to it, and went to a hotel for the night. When I returned the next day, she was waiting for me in the kitchen: with a knife. She lunged towards me, ready to plunge it into my chest, but I caught her hand in time. Then she moved away, and grabbed another knife from the drawer. I thought she was bluffing, and said as much. And then she sliced her wrist open. I've never seen anything like it. We spent that day in hospital. She made me promise not to tell the doctors it was attempted suicide. Stupidly, I agreed, and I've lived to regret it. A pattern was set, and so whenever I mentioned that we needed to move on there'd be some sort of stunt: mock drowning, pills, parking the car at the top of a cliff. Margaret was inventive, I'll give her that much. But it grew tedious. It took the will to live from me.'

'But you haven't lived together for some time. What changed?' Mahalia asked.

'I relocated to Red Maple Manor. It had always been our family's country home, but when my father talked of selling it and retiring to Florida, I said that I wanted it for my main residence. He laughed because it wasn't worth much to him, not compared to all his other properties. But the Manor saved my life. I told her I needed to set up a studio to work with new talent, and it was best to be away from the city for that. The truth is, it's not always convenient being so far away from New York, but I made it work for me. She never argued, and soon I spent more and more of my days and nights there until I was living at the manor full time. It kind of happened organically, really. She hates the country, so it was the perfect bolt-hole for me. I had our Boston home set up with staff so they could cater to her every whim. When I went back to check on the place, just a once-over to check everything was structurally sound, I found her in bed with her personal trainer. Best day of my life, well, one of them! I knew that I could finally put the divorce papers into action. She had moved on, and finally I could do that too. But I guess a personal trainer doesn't come with staff, houses dotted around the country, and a bank account to keep you in the lifestyle you have become accustomed.'

'Beau, I'm so sorry. I wish I'd been more understanding. No wonder you don't want to get married again. I get that now. I don't blame you. I'd feel the same.'

'You would?'

'Yes,' she smiled, and kissed his lips tenderly. Gently placing her palm against his cheek, she whispered: 'I don't need a marriage certificate. I don't need any legal tie to you. I want you, and want to be with you. That's all that matters. And I promise, that no matter what, I'll never do anything to make you stay with me if you don't want to.'

Beau held her close. She didn't need to say those words. He knew that she was nothing like Margaret.

But it was good to hear her say it out loud. A part of him felt like he needed some sort of reassurance.

Café Goddess

'So after your meeting at noon with the editor, what are your plans,' Beau asked.

Mahalia prepared Beau an espresso, and banana and maple pancakes. They were at Citrus Avenue Café, just after dawn, and she was getting ready for the first staff to arrive.

'No plans,' she said, looking up and smiling.

'Will you come back to my place afterwards? Or do you need to come back here?' he asked.

'No, Hestia and Ellie have got this place covered. I just wanted to check up on things this morning. Sure, I'll come over. Shall I pick up some produce to make dinner?'

'That'd be lovely.' Beau looked into her eyes, smiling, 'I was wondering if you might be free to come to the Country Music Awards in Nashville with me next week?'

Mahalia's face lit up. 'I'll make sure I'm free! Are you kidding me? Wow. I'd love to go.'

'That's settled then,' he replied, feeling rather pleased with himself. Beau couldn't imagine what their relationship would be like if they didn't share a love for the same music. Margaret didn't like any music of any description: *irritated her*, she said.

Beau had his coffee, finished reading the paper, and kissed her goodbye. 'I'm going to miss you.' He held her for quite some time, not really ready to let her go.

They'd been inseparable since the day he turned up at her apartment. She sure as hell was going to miss him too. But at least she had plenty to think about.

This was her first face-to-face meeting with the editor, and she was so excited.

After briefing Ellie on the requirements for the week's menu, Mahalia caught a taxi to the airport, and boarded her flight to New York. It was going to be a long day, but one she was looking forward to. It had been hard work to make it this far, and she'd already delivered a huge portfolio of photographs and recipes to the publisher after she'd completed the main manuscript.

Kathryn O'Malley greeted Mahalia in the downstairs foyer of HarperCollins.

'Mahalia, hi! I'm so looking forward to working together. Come upstairs. I've ordered lunch. Are you hungry?'

'I'm always hungry,' she laughed.

They hit it off instantly, like old friends, laughing at all sorts of things. No topics were taboo. Mahalia even found herself confiding about Margaret the Mad Woman.

'Scary! I knew a 'Margaret' once, but her name was Angela. And she was not an angel, but the devil incarnate. Be careful,' she said kindly. 'People like that shouldn't be allowed to walk the streets. Others are fooled by their charm offensive, and have no inkling about the demons lurking just below. Like I said, be careful.'

They got down to business, nibbling at their ploughman's sandwiches, and sipping elderflower presse.

'I love this photo!' Kathryn hooted. 'Is that Beau? God he's hot. No wonder you fell for him! Can we use this?'

Mahalia laughed. 'I wasn't planning to. Really, I was strictly going for photos of the food. I only included the ones of him because they were fun.'

Kathryn's editorial eye disagreed.

'Exactly. See the look on his face? It tells you far more about that minted-chocolate mousse than any description ever could. Seriously, we have to use this. Oh….and *this* one!' she laughed out loud. It was a portrait of Beau eating pumpkin dumplings. 'That's a look of pure ecstasy. Can we get his permission?' Kathryn's excitement was contagious.

Mahalia picked up her cellphone and texted him.

'Sure,' came his brief reply, followed by 'I miss you!'

'That was easy! I'll get the legal paperwork sorted out for his official permission.' Kathryn laughed. 'So you say most of these photos and recipes were taken at his house?'

'Yeah, most of them. There are still some more I'd like to take, but what I'd really love is to do them at my grandfather's old homestead. There's such a lovely rustic feel about the place. That was my original goal: for them to all be done there.' And then she told Kathryn the story of Keith McVeigh, and how Beau rescued her.

'He's a regular superhero! Don't let him go, will ya?'

Mahalia had no intention of letting him go. Not now, not ever.

'We've got the recipes, and all the text laid out. We just need some more photos. My boss would love to have this go to press in October, ready for the Christmas sales. How much longer do you think you need?'

'Wow, the pressure's on! It won't take me too long.'

'Perfect. We can start laying out some of the photos we've got already for the themed aspects, like the foreign-foods section.' And then Kathryn's face lit up. 'We're finishing with recipes of love.'

'You should be publishing romance novels, Kathryn!' Mahalia laughed.

'Love, food, romance. It's all the same to me. As long as it makes you feel good, and makes your pulse race. And makes you sigh!'

'Oh my god, you really should be a romance editor.'

'Actually, I used to be,' Kathryn confided, her tone softening as she reached for Mahalia's hand. 'I loved my job but my husband got relocated, and this was the only editing job I could get. Don't get me wrong, I adore being here. And besides, I'd never have met you if I didn't work here.' She laughed, stood up, and said, 'I'll come to the airport with you.'

They laughed all the way back, until their sides ached; the cab driver quite unclear about what was so darned funny. They were the craziest passengers he'd ever had. Eyes dripping with tears, they hugged goodbye.

'I'll look after your book,' Kathryn promised. 'Just get me the rest of the photos as soon as you can. Don't get too sidetracked by Superman.'

They said goodbye to a final laugh, and Mahalia boarded the plane.

When her thoughts turned to Beau, she suddenly realised she was so exhausted. Even though she'd promised to cook him dinner, the thought of doing that after such a long day seemed too much. It was an hour's drive from the airport to his home in the hills. Maybe she could pick up a takeaway when she got back.

The flight was pleasant, and she made light conversation with a breastfeeding counsellor who was attending a natural-birth conference in Asheville.

'Do you have children?' Lani asked.

'No. Not yet,' and Mahalia's heart fluttered. 'My life's rather too full for children, but...I would have them tomorrow if it were so simple.'

'There's never a perfect time. If your heart is calling you, then maybe you need to listen,' Lani smiled.

'Perhaps you're right.'

They enjoyed the rest of the flight together, and then exchanged email addresses.

Mahalia walked through the arrivals' lounge debating whether to get a cab or a bus back to her apartment. Once there, she'd pick up her truck to drive to the mountains.

A hand lightly touched her shoulder.

'Honey.'

'Beau!' she exclaimed, jumping into his arms. 'You're here!'

'I figured you'd be too tired to drive up to the hills. Let me take you out to dinner. We can stay at your place tonight, and head back to the Manor tomorrow.'

'Perfect. Just perfect. *You're* perfect.'

What a thoughtful thing for him to do: meet her at the airport, and take her to dinner. And take her to bed. She couldn't wait.

'Tell me all about your day. I want to hear about every second of it.'

Mahalia regaled him with stories, and their laughter.

'Superhero, hey? I can live with that,' he laughed.

'You are though, you know? With you by my side, I feel like I can do anything.'

'I'm not taking any credit. Everything you've done, you've done on your own.'

When they arrived back at Mahalia's apartment, she had a quick shower and then went into her bedroom to get dressed. 'Casual or smart?' she called out, when standing in front of her wardrobe.

'Dressy.'

Damn, she said to herself. 'Limited choice I'm afraid.'

But when she emerged wearing a white, fitted, jersey wraparound dress that finished at her ankles, Beau had to catch his breath.

'Wow,' was all he said. 'Wow.'

'Really? I don't have much in the way of fancy clothes. Never been a need for them working such long hours in the café.'

'Well, you make me feel like the proudest man in all of Asheville. Not quite sure we'll make it to the restaurant though,' he groaned when he pulled her close.

'Come on!' Mahalia laughed, dragging him to the door. 'Plenty of time for all that later. I'm hungry!'

'So am I,' he moaned, reluctantly heading down the stairwell. His body ached for her. They'd already been apart for too long.

They listened to some mandolin and fiddle Bluegrass instrumental music on the drive. As Beau pulled into Macon Avenue, Mahalia asked 'Where are we going?'

'The Grove Park Inn. Have you been there before?'

'No, but I've heard fabulous things about it.'

'We're booked into the Sunset Terrace.'

'It's iconic! Upscale. Classic. Emphasis on local foods, award-winning wine list,' she said excitedly, recalling a five-star review.

'Sounds about right,' he laughed. 'My dad used to bring me here a lot. The outdoor terrace offers breathtaking views of the Blue Ridge Mountains. I wanted you to have an evening that you'd never forget. The main inn is about one hundred years old.'

Mahalia looked at him thoughtfully. 'Beau, every evening I have with you is one I'll never forget.'

They were seated, and attended to as if they were the only people in the restaurant. Mahalia rather enjoyed such first-class care. Yep, she could get used to it. They both chose the onion soup au gratin for starters, rich with parmesan, gruyère, provolone and sweet cherry.

'I'm so going to make this in the café! It's exquisite.'

'A bit expensive for a lunchtime menu isn't it?' Beau asked.

'I'll just put the price up!' she replied, matter of factly.

'You really are some businesswoman!' And he sat back in his chair, seeing her in a whole new way.

Together they ate roasted beets with cracked pepper, goat's cheese, pistachios; balsamic chard, squash, red pepper, Portobello mushrooms and soft polenta; Carolina corn and butter-roasted asparagus.

'Please don't ask me to eat dessert,' she pleaded.

'You can fit that in later,' he promised, his suggestion causing her to blush. 'Besides, there's something I want to show you while we're here. Beau led her down to the Dueling Piano Bar.

'This is apparently the most fun you'll have in Asheville on a Friday night.'

The live entertainment had them dancing and singing for hours. Mahalia forgot how tired she was, and had a fantastic time listening to the local comedians.

'We have to come back here again,' she insisted when he led her out to the car. 'And that was just the piano playing. The food was amazing! Thank you so much, Beau.'

'My pleasure, honey. It was all my pleasure. I've got another treat lined up for you.'

'Really, what is it?'

'Have you heard of the Wailin' Jennys?'

'Who hasn't?'

'They're playing in New York soon. I've got front-row tickets and backstage passes.'

'And you're taking me?' she squealed and wrapped her arms around him. 'I can't wait! How fantastic,' she said, giddy with excitement.

'You're so easy to please,' he laughed, squeezing her tightly.

'Oh you're wrong there. I'm not easy to please.'

'Yes you are.' Eight years with Margaret Pilkington-Candler had shown him just how easy it was to be with a woman like Mahalia. Everything about her was trouble free.

Margaret was a give-me, give-me, give-me sort of woman. The worst sort: greedy, selfish, self-centred and demanding. And Mahalia? She was a thank-you woman. Her appreciation for everything in life made him want to give her the best he could. She never asked for anything, never demanded anything from; but always showed gratitude. Mahalia simply didn't take anything in life for granted.

Rattled

'I've got tickets to a new art exhibition on Sunday. Do you fancy a drive down to Asheville with me?' Mahalia asked as she prepared their evening meal.

'I'd love to. Do you know who the artist is?'

'Not personally, no. She's a young Iranian artist, and I've heard great things about her work.' She could see Beau smiling as he read the newspaper. 'What's so funny?' she asked.

'Nothing's funny,' he said, looking up. 'I just love how supportive you are of other people's talent. Even strangers! Not everyone's like that. The world is full of blocked creatives who are quite quick to dismiss other people's art. But you? You celebrate everyone, and I love that about you. I don't know if I've ever met anyone who has been to so many art exhibitions. You're so nurturing.'

'The world is big enough for everyone and their dreams,' she said, kissing him on the forehead. 'We all need encouragement.'

'You smell good,' he replied, breathing in the vanilla and cinnamon of the pear crumble she was making. Beau pulled her a little closer.

'You, Mister, are just going to have to wait!'

But he pulled her closer anyway. Beau wanted her, and he didn't want to wait. Dessert could wait. Beau lifted her up onto the kitchen counter, and moved away the vase of flowers. If the pear crumble could have blushed, it would have.

On Sunday morning, Mahalia was up at first light, mounting Carolina Blue and riding the mare up to the ridge. She circled down past her grandfather's old house, and came back to Red Maple Manor just as Beau was making coffee.

'Good timing!' he said, greeting her with a warm hug. 'What time do you want to head to the exhibition?'

'Straight after I have a shower.'

As they drove down the mountain, Beau played her some recent recordings of Lola and Russ.

'She's really going to go a long way,' Mahalia mused. 'There's something so original about her sound. Once you've heard her voice, you could never forget it. You know, she's lucky to have you, Beau. Someone as young as Lola needs a nurturing father figure to guide her through this industry.'

'I'm not that old!' he laughed.

There was already quite a crowd at the gallery, and Mahalia recognised a few faces from other exhibitions and introduced Beau to the Jensens, Rolands, Estés family and Thompsons.

'Is there anyone you don't know in Asheville?' he chuckled.

'Loads!' she laughed. 'I only know these people from chatting at exhibitions, and then later on from them recognising me when they came into the café. I like people, and I make sure I remember their names, where they're from, and how we met.'

'That sounds just like you,' he said, wrapping his arms around her.

'Not here,' she whispered as he kissed her intimately.

'What? I'm not allowed to ravish you in public? Not allowed to unbutton your blouse and take you right here, right now?'

'Beau,' she whispered, her breathing rapid. Every inch of her body was arguing with logic.

Beau smiled, and reached for her hand. 'What do you think of this piece?' he asked, changing the subject, and looking at the figure of a young woman nursing a baby against the backdrop of a lighthouse.

'I find it quite moving. You can see she's devoted to her baby, and there's a sense of her being like an island in the world. When I look at it I wonder what the lighthouse is representing? Has it protected her from the rocky cliffs? Or is she waiting for her lover to return from the sea? Maybe he died at sea, and she's waiting there until the end of time?'

Beau looked at her. 'Do you always put so much thought into a piece of art?'

'Yes,' she said matter of factly. 'I do. Art is telling a story, and if there are no words there to tell me what it's about, then I create them. I become the storyteller.'

'Have you ever thought of writing novels?' He asked the question as a joke, but no sooner were the words out of his mouth he could tell the cogs were turning in her brain, considering it as a viable creative career option.

'The Lighthouse Lady,' she said, more to herself than to Beau. 'I'll give that some thought.'

Was she serious? That's what he loved about her. Nothing, nothing at all, was off limits to her. Mahalia grabbed life with both hands. No wonder he fell in love. She was like sunshine in his life, brightening up even the darkest of wintry corners. Of all the things in this world that he could buy, she wasn't one of them.

And that was what made her invaluable. Mahalia was priceless. It scared the life out of him. There was no insurance that she'd stay. She, Mahalia Mason, was the greatest gamble of his life.

'Mahalia?' an enthusiastic voice came from behind her. It was a voice from her past. A voice which had initially brought happiness, and then confusion. She turned around slowly. *Not here, Brad, not now*, she pleaded in her mind. But it was too late.

'Brad,' she said politely, smiling and acting pleased. 'How nice to see you.'

Although he looked well, and devilishly handsome, she didn't want to think about that part of her life. She was content with Beau, and didn't need reminding of a time when she doubted who she was as a woman.

Brad reached forward to hug her, and held on far too long for either her or Beau's liking.

'This is my…this is Beau. Beau Candler.'

'Beau, this is Brad.'

Brad reached out his hand to Beau.

'Brad and I knew each other a number of years ago,' she explained.

Brad snickered in disbelief. 'It was a little bit more than that! I courted you for four years, Mahalia. I chased you relentlessly across Asheville for four *very long* years. I tried every trick in the book to get you to marry me. Or have you forgotten?'

She blushed. Of course she hadn't forgotten!

Beau's blood was beginning to boil. Brad's hands were *still* on Mahalia's shoulders, trying to hold her in position, like an insect being held down by a scientist's pins and being studied in great detail.

102

When Mahalia reached out for Beau's hand, he gently prised her away from the tense situation she was in.

Brad stepped back in observation of the not-so-subtle cue.

'I should never have let you walk away,' he said softly, taking in her beauty. 'You were the best thing that ever happened to me. You look fantastic. Time has worn well on you. What are you doing these days? How are you?'

Beau wanted to punch him then and there. How dare Brad declare something so intimate to her in front of him?

'As I recall, Brad, it was *you* who walked away. It was you who found me lacking in some way.' She was firm in her reply.

'No, it was you. You walked away,' he argued. 'I would never have left a beauty like you.'

Mahalia wasn't about to argue. The sooner they finished this conversation, the better.

Beau let go of her hand and moved on to another painting. He couldn't stand the way Brad claimed ownership of Mahalia.

She watched him walk away, and panicked.

'Nice seeing you Brad. Take care,' and she left him abruptly and put her hand in Beau's when she caught up to him.

'I'm so sorry, Beau. There's no excuse for him talking to me like that in front of you.'

'Perhaps if you'd introduced me as your other half he might not have treated me like I was your neighbour.'

Instantly she was relieved to see a small smile on his lips.

'I don't know what to call you. How do I introduce you? My lover? My boyfriend? My partner?'

'Your man,' he chuckled. 'Or Superman! Either is fine by me.'

'Okay.' She walked alongside of him. 'Okay, Superman it is.' They both chuckled, and squeezed each other's hand tightly, relieved to be away from Brad.

'I thought...You told me there'd never been anyone serious. You said you'd never had sex before. How could you have been with him for *four* years? How could he have been with *you* for four years and leave you alone? I can't comprehend how any red-blooded man could do that? How could any man survive you? And why does he look at you with such devotion? And...why did you have such pain in your eyes? Why did he leave you? I assume he had a good reason.'

'Pain? Well, because I came out of that relationship wondering if there was something wrong with me. Brad was always so frustrated that I was a content woman who didn't fall madly head-over-heels in love with him, or any man for that matter. He said it wasn't natural for a woman not to be dreaming about wedding dresses and children.'

'You didn't want to get married?'

'Not to him, I guess. I loved my life. I loved my friends, my social life, and my balcony full of herbs. I would rather have spent a Sunday afternoon watering basil and strumming my guitar than watching yet another horror movie with him. I have always been happy in my own company, and he just couldn't get that. He thought there was something psychologically wrong with me, and by the end of our relationship I started to wonder if he was right. The pain you saw has nothing to do with not being with him. I was glad to walk away: one of the best decisions of my life. The pain was that I let someone's misunderstanding of me erode my confidence as a woman. And Brad? He'd have married me in a heartbeat. But it was he who walked away, really. Not me. He walked away every time he criticised me. Every time he devalued how I spent my leisure time. In the end, I simply reclaimed myself and said "enough". If he chooses to see that as me walking away, then fair enough. But we both know the truth: I wasn't good enough for him.'

'By the look in his eyes, he would still marry you!'

'Yeah. I guess I did break his heart.'

'Why didn't you have sex with him?'

'Because that's all it would have been. I wasn't going to open my legs just to satisfy his urges. Lovemaking is sacred, and...you probably think I sound stupid.' Mahalia looked to the floor, realising she'd made Beau the altar of her devotion, and the huge responsibility which she placed on him by being the first man.

'Nothing you say ever sounds stupid,' he said, and drew her into a hug. Beau reached down and kissed her slowly, passionately. They lingered over each other, wanting more, tempting, teasing, promising. *Later*, they whispered to each other. Beau was acutely aware that Brad was looking on, but that wasn't his motivation for sweeping Mahalia off her feet just then. It was merely a bonus. He scooped her up, lifted her into the air, swung her around, then placed her back on her feet. 'I love you just the way you are.'

They bumped into Brad later on in the gallery, and he asked, somewhat nervously, 'So you two are seeing each other?'

'Yes. We live together. We're very much a couple.' And as she said those words so confidently, so brightly,

Beau squeezed her hand just that little bit tighter.

That's my girl. You tell him!

'Glad to see you so happy Mahalia,' Brad said, but she knew him well enough to know that they were just words. He was simply being his charming self. Charm, but no substance. And in that revelatory moment, she realised it was one of the things she truly loved about Beau: that they could delve into their deepest feelings and thoughts with each other, without any fear of rejection or criticism. They always came together in a spirit of honesty, intimacy, tenderness and openness. That had made all the difference.

As Brad walked away, Beau said, 'You know, I love that about you.'

'What? What do you love?'

'That you're self-contained. That you don't actually need me or anyone else. It's refreshing. Disturbing, sometimes, that you could just walk away, but always refreshing.'

'But you're wrong, Beau. I need you. I really need you.'

'Later,' he laughed, but they both knew that it was time to leave the gallery. They headed back to her Asheville apartment. It would take far too long to get back to Red Maple Manor! Especially now. Especially now when she *needed* him!

They barely had a foot in the front door when their clothes were discarded and Beau picked her up and carried her straight to the bedroom.

'You need me, hey? Good!'

After Beau placed her on the bed, he stood up to remove the last of his clothing. 'I love you Mahalia. You know that, don't you?'

'Of course I know that!' she said. 'Why are you

saying it so seriously?'

'I just want to be sure. I don't want you to ever think I take you for granted.'

'Make love with me Beau. Stop talking!' she laughed.

He climbed onto the bed and tickled her.

'Stop it,' she squealed. 'You know I hate being tickled.'

'So you say!' He stopped and wrapped his arms around her. 'You are the most gorgeous creature on the planet. And you're with me...'

'Don't you ever forget it!' she said, tickling him back.

Beau's deepest desire was to melt into Mahalia, to become one with her, in every way possible.

'You are the love of my life, Mahalia. You have made my life. I want you to know that. I'm sorry that you didn't know how to introduce me today. What we have isn't fleeting. It's not going to be over next week or next year. I'm here for the long haul.'

'Jeez, I hope it's not a haul!' and her smile let him know that she was in for a lifetime too.

They made love slowly that lazy Sunday afternoon. Every touch of her skin; the way she smelled of Summer and arousal, of peaches and vanilla coffee, had him aching for more. The sounds of her pleasure brought him closer to her, and despite their serene touch and gentle movements, they eventually climaxed with the grace of a ballerina pirouetting upon a precarious mountain-top crevice. Beautiful and crazy! It made them laugh out loud, when at that very moment of bodily triumph, exaltation and excruciating pleasure, a clap of thunder echoed across the city.

The Alphabet

They were seated in Beau's private plane, and flew out of Asheville airport first thing that morning.

'I can't believe I'm actually going to the Country Music Awards. This is so exciting!' Mahalia said, her squeals of delight catching Beau by surprise.

'They're a lot of fun. I'm glad that we're sharing it together.'

Beau and Mahalia sipped coffee, and held hands.

'Where are we staying?' she asked.

'Loews Vanderbilt. The hotel is quite near to the downtown attractions, and across the street from the University campus. I reckon you'll like the feel of the place.'

'I just can't believe I'm going to be there. I've always dreamed of this. Beau, thank you so much,' she smiled, feeling like a little girl on Christmas morning.

The cab driver drove them the twelve-mile journey to the hotel.

'This is Music Row,' Beau said, 'and there's the Country Music Hall of Fame.'

When the driver pulled up outside the hotel, Mahalia immediately recognised it as five-star luxury accommodation, but then she wouldn't have expected Beau to stay anywhere else. Comfort was in his blood. It was something that was quickly seeping into hers, and she had to admit that she rather enjoyed being pampered.

Mahalia looked all around the reception area, with its tall marble pillars and huge floral displays.

'Enough flowers for you?' Beau chuckled.

'I think so. This is amazing. Beau, thank you so much. I can't believe I'm here. In Nashville!'

Popular country songs played on the sound system, and various memorabilia from celebrities hung throughout the vogue-look hotel.

Once they were in their suite, Mahalia lay back on the bed. The frame was made from dark cherry wood, and matched the rest of the furniture.

'This is fun,' she said.

'What is?' Beau asked.

'Being away with you!' She picked up the hotel's information brochure, and read through the facilities on offer. 'This is a rather eclectic menu.'

'So, do you want to eat in the hotel, or should we go somewhere else?'

'Here is fine by me. I'll just get changed.' Mahalia stepped into the shower, and let the long flight drain away as she washed her hair.

Later, as they sat down in one of the hotel's restaurants, Beau remarked on how full of energy Mahalia looked. 'I thought you'd be tired after the long journey.'

'I was, but now I could just go out dancing all night. It's so exciting to be here. It feels like the opportunity of a lifetime.'

Thrilled by her excitement, he said 'I hope you'll feel that way next year, and the year after that...'

'I'm sure it will feel like the first time every time we come back here!'

'I'll take you to the Hall of Fame tomorrow during the day, and we'll go to the awards tomorrow night.'

The waiter brought a menu for them to study while they sipped wine.

Mahalia heard Beau groan with displeasure.

'What's wrong, honey?' Mahalia asked, surprised to see their pleasant evening shift gears.

'Someone I'd rather not see has just seen me. And she's coming this way. Tighten your seatbelt.'

'Beau Candler, I do declare. How wonderful to see you!'

'Arabella,' he said, standing like a gentleman and briefly kissing her cheek. 'How are you?' He didn't want to know the answer to that, and certainly didn't care whether she was well or not. No, not at all. Beau Candler just wanted her gone, and preferably as quickly as possible.

'All the better for seeing you,' she swooned, her short black hair swishing around her square chin. 'Oh my, you look just as devastatingly gorgeous as ever. You've always been so sexy!' she purred, and rubbed her hand on his shoulder far too long for his liking. For a moment, he wondered if Mahalia might have a jealous rage but she looked rather amused at the situation and then stood up and introduced herself.

'Hello Arabella. I'm Mahalia, Beau's partner.'

'Business partner?' she enquired, looking Mahalia up and down rather slowly. Despite Mahalia's clothes being more than adequate for the occasion, there was something about her that showed she was wild at heart, and not a woman who could be domesticated to fit into the society pages.

'No, *life* partner.' Mahalia sat back down in her chair, and sipped some more wine.

Beau loved her for that! Not entirely sure how he was going to get Arabella Blease's claws out of him, he decided to follow Mahalia's lead; she didn't seem the slightest bit bothered by the woman's presence.

'Do you live around here?' Mahalia asked casually.

'Boston. Beau and I dated in Boston. But I'm sure he's told you all that,' and her self-satisfied smugness only ignited Mahalia's playfulness. She'd already spent more than enough time with Beau's wife to be extremely intolerant of any other woman who presumed ownership of him. Where did he find these women? What was he thinking? She shuddered. Nope, this was not the time to be a good girl. There was only one thing for it: the time was right for Mahalia *bad-ass* Mason.

'Well, you know Beau,' she said, raising her eyebrows. 'He has women falling over him all the time.' Mahalia spoke in exaggerated tones, deliberately making her almond-shaped eyes even larger.

It was all Beau could do not to laugh out loud. He'd never seen her like this before: Queen of Storytelling. 'I really can't keep track of everyone: Anna, Barbara, Carrie, Denise, Eloise, Fenella, Gloria, Hatti, Ingrid, Juliet, Karen...' she waved her arms as if describing the whole world. 'There's an entire alphabet of women with a claim to Beau. He's such a Casanova! But I guess that's what makes him such an incredible lover. How could he not be with all that experience?'

Beau nearly choked on his wine. How could she be so cool and collected about it all? He looked back and forward between both women. Mahalia was relaxed, kind, charming, and Arabella was incandescent with rage.

'So...' Arabella said, trying to gather her thoughts. 'Are you two serious? Or are you just part of Beau's *alphabet*?'

'I'm Z. It all ends with me,' she smiled gently, then

turned to Beau. 'I get the benefit of all his mistakes and experience. I really think we should order some more of this wine, honey. What do you think? Maybe we could get some bottles to take back home to North Carolina.'

Beau joined in the game.

'Anything for you, my love.' Beau reached over and held her hand. There wasn't a single woman he'd ever met who could have pulled off the evening like Mahalia had.

'Arabella, are you dining alone, or you would you like to join Beau and I?'

'Thank you, but I'm here with friends...for the Country Music Awards. Beau used to talk so highly of them, that I thought I'd see them for myself.'

'What? Beau never took you to the awards?' She looked at him in mock horror. 'I just assumed you brought all your girlfriends here. Honey, what were you thinking not bringing her here?'

'We didn't date long enough for me to invite her,' and he hoped with all his heart that Arabella would take the hint and leave. 'We dated for, what was it? One week?'

Arabella looked uncomfortable. It was true. They'd dated for one week, and only had one date. It had been the longest evening of his life, and he'd been bored out of his brain. Sure, she was attractive, but it was only skin deep.

'Do come and visit us in North Carolina if you're ever over that way, Arabella. We have plenty of space for guests.' Mahalia stood up, and reached over to kiss her. As she moved in to embrace her, she winked at Beau. It was hard for him to keep a straight face.

'See you again!' Mahalia called out cheerily after her as she walked away. 'Funny, Beau, I'd never have

112

picked her as your type. Where do you find such women? Really, your taste was pretty poor before I came along. I'm so hungry. Let's order.'

'How did you do that? How did you not let her rile you? How did you...'

'How did I what?'

'I thought you might have been jealous.'

'Of her?'

'Well, of her and I.'

'Did you love her? Did you make love to her like you make love to me? Did you live with her? Did she break your heart?'

'Er, no. No. No. And that last one would be no as well. We never made love...or even had *sex*.'

'Do you want to be with her now?'

'No!'

'So there's nothing for me to be jealous of. Right here, right now, you're with me. Tonight, I'm the woman in your bed, and I'm sure as hell going to be the last thing you think of when you fall asleep and the first thing you think of when you wake up.'

'I love that about you! You're so damn confident about us.'

'I'm confident about who I am. If I wasn't, then we wouldn't work. It's really that simple.'

'I hope she doesn't take you up on your offer to visit us.'

'She won't, you can be sure of that.'

'What is my type, by the way?'

'Me,' she said, smiling as she perused the menu. 'Only me.'

'Now there's a woman you might like to meet,' he whispered.

Mahalia looked up and gasped. 'Carrie Underwood.'

'Would you like me to introduce you?' he offered.

'Of course!' Then her face turned a little serious. 'You haven't dated her, have you?'

He laughed. 'No!'

'Good, because I would be jealous!'

As the evening wore on, Mahalia continued to feel elated. Names she'd listened to singing her favourite songs, were all in town for the awards.

'Keith Urban,' she said. 'I have to meet him. Do you think he'll mind?'

'Hardly. He's a friend of mine. We've stayed at each other's homes.'

Beau was a member of the CMA, and a ballot voter of the awards. It wasn't surprising he knew so many people, but it was a whole new side to him that Mahalia was seeing. She knew Beau as the man tucked away in the mountains, sitting beneath headphones and making life-changing decisions for artists. Tonight he was animated and laughing, catching up with people he'd known for years. People he clearly considered as friends.

Mahalia was totally swept away by the Southern charm and hospitality, and the rich celebrity culture of the country-music industry.

The awards were more than she could have hoped for. The music was spectacular, the honours were well deserved. A dream came true when Beau took her back stage and introduced her to the legendary King of Country, Garth Brooks, and then later to the Mavericks and Lonestar.

'I'm awestruck. I'm not entirely sure I want to go back to reality. This has been so much fun.'

'We can do it all again next year,' Beau promised. 'And the next…'

Sisters

Beau had just returned from a meeting when he walked in on Mahalia in the kitchen at Red Maple Manor. He couldn't help smile when he overheard her on the phone to her sister. They spoke every other day, and he wondered how they could find so much to talk about: every single time. *Girls*, he laughed. And in that moment Beau wondered what it would be like to have daughters, and if he ever did he hoped the bond would be as great as the one between Mahalia and Anita. They were the best of friends.

Anita was three years younger than Mahalia, and had spent the past five years working her way around Australia. Not a week went by when there wasn't a postcard or five-page letter coming through the post, or gifts of boomerangs and gum-nut earrings or other such touristy gimmicks.

What really made him laugh was just how excited Mahalia was when she opened the packets.

They'd always been close, but when she reached eighteen and received a living inheritance from her grandfather, Anita chose to spread her wings and see the world. The money ran out fairly quickly, as she lived the high life, but she fell in love with Australia and decided to stay, even though it meant working for a living.

For Mahalia, it had been a long few years apart. Their parents, born and bred in Asheville, had moved to Canada around the same time, and bought a small bed and breakfast on a peach farm in Okanagan. They were settled and happy.

'Hey guess what?' Mahalia called out to Beau, her face alive with joy. 'Anita's coming home! I can't believe it. You'll love her! That girl has more life than anyone I know. She's such fun.'

'More life than you?' he chuckled. 'Is that actually possible?'

'Am I lively?' she asked seriously.

Beau picked her up in his arms, and carried her upstairs.

'Oh yes my darling, you are lively.'

She giggled as he kissed her neck.

'Where will she be staying? Is she coming to Asheville?'

'Yes! I guess she could stay in my apartment, or...'

'Or *here*?'

'No, I was going to say my grandfather's place.'

He laughed. 'Would I ever see you again if she was living that close?'

'Yes!'

'His house is still in your name Mahalia. I didn't change it over.'

'But...the money? The money was transferred to my account.'

'The property needs a lot of work. You should use it for repairs.'

'But it's your money.'

'Ours. It's ours. And the roof needs replacing, and the verandah could be redone too. And the barn, and the kitchen.'

'I'm getting the message!' and she squeezed him tightly. 'Thank you!' They lay on the bed, and despite his original intentions when he brought Mahalia up the stairs, they ended up talking for hours. He had to laugh to himself. Who was he to think Mahalia and Anita always had so much to talk about? It was no different for him. Mahalia was such a good listener, and always so interested in what he had to say, and how he felt, and what he thought about things, about life, about people. Always curious; never tired of asking questions. She was easy to talk to, and he'd never experienced a relationship like this before: easy companionship.

'Kathryn thinks the book is going to be really popular. I was wondering about turning grandfather's house into a cookery retreat...just small intimate courses. I'd still retain ownership of the café, but would spend most of my time teaching.'

'Anything that has you closer to me suits me just fine. Do you think you might sell your apartment, or rent it out? I mean, we are living together now, aren't we?' he asked.

'Yes, we are. Are you okay with that? Do you feel *trapped*?' she teased, tickling him.

Beau climbed over Mahalia and pinned her arms down.

'Do *you* feel trapped?' he growled into her hair.

'Deliciously so,' she swooned.

'Me too.'

Beau awoke to find the bed empty. Perhaps Mahalia was in the kitchen making breakfast. But when he got down there were no delicious smells to greet him. Just a note:

Taken Carolina Blue for a ride.
Back in an hour or so. Love, M.

It warmed his heart that she'd gotten back into horse riding again with such a passion. His eight-year abiding memory was of her on the back of a horse. Might as well go back to bed, he thought.

When he opened the curtains on the balcony, he

could see a figure on horseback down by the church house. One look at that flaming copper hair told him exactly where she was. He watched her dismount, and walk amongst the headstones; the horse following her. For a few minutes, she stood in front of her grandfather's headstone, and then knelt down.

It occurred to Beau that they'd never had a conversation about how her Granddad Jack's death had impacted her. They were close, he knew that; she'd spent every one of her school holidays with him, chatting on the verandah, helping him grow vegetables, riding his horse: Old Blue. Beau quickly changed, and ran out to saddle up Tonto, his paint-coloured stallion.

With no time to waste, he galloped up the drive and down the river road to the church. When he arrived, she was still there, arranging a small posy of tall bellflowers by the grave. Carolina Blue was eating grass as if she had all the time in the world.

'Honey,' he said, approaching her quietly.

'Beau? Hi. What are you doing here?'

'Just wanted to check you were alright.'

'I'm fine sweetheart. I was just saying "hello" to granddad.'

'Do you miss him?'

'More than you could imagine. He was always there for me. My parents were great, but he seemed to really understand my....' But she couldn't find the word.

'Passion?' he laughed.

'Yes, you could call it that. Some people thought I was feisty, but it wasn't that. I just felt so alive. School was like a straightjacket. I wanted freedom to experience all of life. Granddad understood that.'

'Jack wanted us to be together. He knew it could

119

never happen back then, but it was like he had a sixth sense.'

'What do you mean?'

'He took me to one side and told me to be patient. He would always say that it would be worth the wait; that he recognised true love when he saw it.'

'Granddad said that to you?' A small tear fell from her eye. 'He listened to me for hours, days actually, recount every detail of our horseback ride down the mountain, and the colour of your eyes, and the soft curl of your dark hair. How you made me laugh. And how, when you looked into my eyes, it was like I'd found a missing part of myself. I lived a lifetime in that hour.'

'Jack got more than he bargained for then, because he had to listen to me wax lyrical about your copper curls, and freckled nose. It nearly killed me when he said you'd gone away to culinary school. It meant that you wouldn't be coming back in the holidays.'

Beau kissed her on the forehead. 'It all seems like so long ago.'

'In some ways, and not in other ways.'

'Fancy taking a ride up to where we first met?' he asked, reaching for her hand.

Mahalia's face lit up. 'I'd love that! Let's go.'

They rode steadily for an hour or more, and Beau was quite relieved when she pulled some cookies and apples out from her small backpack.

'Hungry?' she asked.

'Starving! I've never thought about food so much in my life since you arrived.'

They ambled up the narrow dirt track, the dappled sunlight falling onto them, and weaved their way among green ash trees and black alder. Nearer to the top of the ridge they reached a forest of Eastern red cedar interspersed with Virginia pine.

'I want to show you something,' Beau said, leading her to an old pine tree.

She gasped with delight when she read the words *Mahalia and Beau forever* scratched into the bark. 'A sweetheart tree! When did you do that?'

'That day. After I left, I rode back up here. I wanted a marker of how I felt,' he admitted. 'Just something tangible that what I felt inside was real.'

'So real you married someone else not much later!' she said sharply.

'I'm with you *now*, Mahalia. That's what matters.'

'I was an adult by the time you married her. Couldn't you have just waited for me? If you felt so strongly, why didn't you track me down at culinary school? I'd have dropped everything for you Beau Candler. *Everything*.'

'I should have, but the truth is I didn't think you'd...'

Mahalia finished the sentence for him: 'Fit into your world?'

'Something like that.'

Mahalia dismounted, and left her horse to graze.

'The air smells so good up here,' Mahalia said, breathing in deeply.

'So, what were you doing up here that day when we first met?' Beau asked curiously.

'Thinking about my life. Deciding who I wanted to be when I grew up! But of course, one look at you when you entered the clearing had every such thought vanish. I wanted to grow up, right then and there, but not because of any job! I wanted... Well, you know what I wanted. Life is cruel sometimes, isn't it?'

'Sure did feel like it! But look at us now. Things are great. We couldn't be happier. Could we?'

'Everything's perfect.'

They tied the horses up, and walked around. After a while, they sat near a fallen log and lay down together. The electricity they felt eight years ago was just as strong.

'I have to ask you something Beau. Tell me the truth.'

A moment of panic caused his heart to beat rapidly. Guilt? But he couldn't think why.

'Okay.'

'The night I moved in and came to your house, there were flowers in the guest room. But you didn't have any guests. Did,' oh how she hated to even ask the question, 'you set Keith up to corner me so you could rescue me and bring me back to your place?' There. It was out. She'd said it. For better or worse.

'Of course I didn't set him up!'

'You didn't?'

'No! I knew you'd just moved in, and I had high hopes of bringing you back home, but I lost my nerve to even go and see you. I was in the kitchen, and saw Keith's tractor speed by the bottom paddock, and I panicked. I waited about five minutes, then I knew, just knew, I had to come over. That's the honest truth, sweetheart.' Beau kissed her tenderly, and for a moment wondered if they'd make love there in the morning sunshine.

'I remembered you loved flowers. The day we met you had them in your hair: nodding onion flower. And bulging from your pocket was a bouquet of purple flox, Indian paintbrush and butterfly weed.'

'You remember all of them?' She was astonished.

'I remember everything, but mostly because you

gave me a lecture on the growing cycle of each one, and how long they flowered for, and the best habitat for them to grow. You turned me into a walking encyclopaedia of wildflowers!'

They leaned in a little closer to each other.

'Your grandfather's verandah had no less than a dozen old glass jam jars filled to the brim with wildflowers. Even his metal milk pale was filled with flowers! Let me see. There was yellow fringed orchid, bluebead lily, mountain laurel, larkspur, columbine and... crested iris.'

'Wow,' she said. 'You're good. Have you got a photographic memory?'

'No, just a good memory! When I commented on the flowers, you said you wanted to be a florist!' Beau chuckled, and said 'An hour later you were tossing pancakes in your grandfather's kitchen and said you wanted to be a chef. You fed me so many I could barely move afterwards. I knew then and there you were a woman who was going to live life fully. And I wanted to share in that zest for life. I'd never met anyone like you before, and I knew that I never would again. You stole my heart.'

'But I wasn't a woman, was I? I was a girl,' she sighed.

'Then your grandfather's kitten walked in and you said wanted to be a mother,' Beau laughed.

'And then *you* went back to the Manor, and I picked another bunch of flowers: bleeding heart! Poor granddad. That really brought a tear to his eye!'

'I found everything about you endearing. So when you moved back here, the way I played it out in my head was that you'd come to dinner, stay late into the night, and I'd offer you the guest bedroom. There would be no catch! I had nothing to do with Keith McVeigh, and I certainly didn't expect to end up in your bed.'

And just the memory of that night had them coming in even closer to each other. The morning sunshine filled them with memories of flowers and horses; it gave them a chance to make new ones. They made love, and the horses ate grass. It wasn't until the Sun was high overhead, at midday, did they get dressed and ride back down the mountain.

Mahalia was so excited about the Wailin' Jennys concert.

'I don't need you to buy me clothes, Beau. I've got enough,' she said as they walked through New York's boutique-laden streets.

'I want to spoil you. Let me buy you some dresses. Please. Do it for me.'

'You spoil me just by being with me, Beau. I don't need more than that. Honestly.'

'And that is what I love about you! Now, stop arguing. Here, let's go in here.'

And just then, Mahalia stepped into a world where she was treated like a queen. In all truth, she found it more than a bit disconcerting and would have preferred to have looked through the clothes on her own rather than have assistants bending over backwards to please her.

Beau sat on a seat in the corner, a smile on his lips. He could see Mahalia was uncomfortable, but he was determined that she came away with clothing that made her feel like a Goddess. She certainly looked like one regardless of what she was wearing.

'Sorry Beau, but there's nothing in here that grabs

my eye,' she said to the horror of the attentive assistants. 'Perhaps we can try somewhere else? Are you bored? It can't be much fun watching me try on dresses.'

'Actually, it's more enjoyable than you could imagine.'

They took their time walking through New York City's opulent stretches of real estate. Even the pavement smelt of luxury.

'I'm a bit hungry, though. Let's have a bite to eat,' he suggested.

When he said that, she thought they'd grab something from a sidewalk vendor, but no, this was Beau Candler. Of course he didn't mean that. Before long, they were in Armani's Fifth Avenue shop at the in-house restaurant: Michelin-starred fine Italian cuisine.

Mahalia absorbed the ambience of their surroundings and impeccable service, being waited on by no less than three people.

Some bite to eat, she thought, savouring every mouthful. She finished a second glass of wine and bowl of Italy's finest pasta. When they headed back into the street, she kept disappearing into one-of-a-kind vintage shops. Not what Beau had in mind, but Mahalia was happy and kept finding 'must have' pieces.

They turned into Greene Street, and Beau said 'One more boutique of my choice. I promise you'll find something here. The owner is like you: she doesn't eat animals.'

'Stella? Stella McCartney?' Mahalia was bowled over and let out an excited squeal as she stepped into the luxurious SoHo two-story boutique.

'This is wonderful, Beau. Simply wonderful! And it's so beautiful in here. Friendly, modern, fashionable.'

'Yes, it's all that, but can you find something you want to wear?'

And she did. Within about one minute. It was ethereal, feminine and was designed as if it only had Mahalia's name on it.

'Sold,' he said.

Afterwards, he showed Mahalia his New York apartment. It was the epitome of luxury and elegance, though Mahalia thought it could do with some photos!

'The views...they're stunning,' was all she could say. 'Why do you keep this place if you're never here?'

'I'm here now, and I use it from time to time for business' he smiled, taking off his suit. She knew that look in his eyes.

'Come here gorgeous! I've spent far too much of this day looking at you, wanting you. Now I want to touch you.'

It was her every pleasure to be held in his strong arms, and to breathe him in. Beau was salty and earthy, and his chest so strong and safe; her fingers felt their way through his dark chest hair, and touched his strong jaw. If there was ever such a thing as a perfect death, it would be this: to die in his arms, her head on his chest, listening to his beating heart.

Desirous for each other, they travelled into the heart of passion: like fireworks exploding all around them. It catapulted them to the stars, and slowly, slowly they came back to Earth, one galaxy at a time.

They showered, and dressed for dinner and the Wailin' Jennys concert.

'I never want us to end, Beau. I love us. I love our life. I love you.'

'Nothing will change that,' he promised.

The chemistry of the band was incredible. Original songs with variety and soul-touching instrumentation: guitar, accordion, banjo, bodhrán, harmonica, drums, ukulele. Their vocals left both Mahalia and Beau with glistening eyes.

'Now *that's* music,' he whispered, after their first song.

Afterwards Mahalia said, 'Would you mind if we stay here, in New York, for a couple more days? It would save me coming back again to meet Anita off the plane.'

'No problem at all. Bill's looking after the horses, and Bessie will keep an eye on the house when she comes to clean. There's no reason why we can't stay.'

'You're coming to the airport with me, right?' she asked, concerned that he was going to linger over his second cup of coffee all morning.

'Yes. I'm coming. We've got plenty of time.' He looked up at her. 'You want to go now? You'd rather sit in an airport for three hours waiting in crowds than sit here in comfort?'

'I'm just so excited!'

Beau stood up. 'Of course you are. Come on then,' he said, taking his cup to the sink.

Mahalia paced the arrivals' lounge, and left Beau to read the New York Times. The plane had landed thirty minutes ago. Anita would be coming through the doors any minute. Mahalia had played this moment out for years. They'd hug, they'd laugh, they'd cry, they'd look each other up and down and jump with excitement.

Mahalia at 5'9", and her long corkscrew copper curls; Anita, just 5'3" and short, straight, baby-blonde hair. Oh yes, they'd hug and scream with delight.

Tears streamed down her eyes. It was all too much. She couldn't wait any longer.

'She'll be out in about five minutes,' Beau said kindly. 'The baggage carousel can be a bit slow and encumbered.'

'You think I'm being impatient?'

'I think you really want to see your little sister!' he laughed, and folded up his paper.

'You know, I haven't seen a photo of her in over a year. She stopped Skyping a while back because of a dodgy broadband connection while she worked as a jillaroo in the Outback. I don't even know what her hair will be like now.'

'She'll look just the same as ever. It'll be like looking in a mirror, minus the copper curls.'

'I'll bet her tan will be amazing from all the Aussie sunshine.'

Passengers from Flight 345 from Melbourne, Australia started filing out. With each new face that came around the door, Mahalia was on tiptoes, straining her neck, looking for her baby sister. She squeezed Beau's hand tightly. Hundreds of people eventually filed through the doors.

'I hope she didn't miss the flight,' Mahalia said, her shoulders sinking. 'What if she tried phoning me, but couldn't get me because I was in New York rather than North Carolina?'

'Not everyone is through yet, honey. Be patient.'

There were families with tired, crying children, and elderly people with walking sticks. An attendant came through pushing a woman in a wheelchair, accompanied by two nurses, and another attendant pushed a luggage trolley. Several flight stewards came through with their baggage, laughing and joking despite being exhausted from the long-haul flight. Mahalia looked beyond them, hoping that Anita would be the next person through. Again, she stood on tiptoes hoping to see behind them. Anita was quite short so she was probably hiding behind someone and going to jump out at the last minute and surprise her. Mahalia felt Beau's hand squeeze hers.

'She's here, honey,' he said in a voice so soft and low that she barely heard him.

'Where? I can't see her.' She jumped up, trying to look above the crowd.

'In the wheelchair,' he said gravely.

'What?' And then Mahalia recognised her eyes. *Anita's eyes*. They locked onto each other. But…but why was she wearing a scarf over her head? Why was she being pushed in a wheelchair?

'Sis?' she asked, tears filling her eyes, as she ran closer to her. Mahalia dropped to her knees in front of her. This wasn't the reunion she'd planned. This wasn't how they were supposed to greet each other.

'What's wrong? Anita, what's wrong? Tell me!'

'Take me home, Hali. Just take me home.' Desperate tears trickled down her sallow cheeks. They weren't tanned as Mahalia expected them to be; they were white and sickly.

Beau and Anita acknowledged each other. There'd be time for introductions once they were out of the public space. Mahalia pushed Anita over to a quiet area, and Beau stood to one side and spoke with the nurses. He took instructions, medication, and a very deep breath at Mahalia's life-changing news, and then pushed the trolley with her suitcases.

'I think we should stay in New York overnight, and then head back to Asheville tomorrow or the next day. You need to rest,' Beau said firmly, as he wheeled Anita into his apartment.

'Hali, sit down,' Anita said as they made their way to the sofas. Beau's apartment was sleek and modern, minimalist and white. It was light and airy, and the design was all based around the skyline views.

'You're sick?' Mahalia said, feeling foolish for stating the obvious. 'You've not said anything in any of our phone calls. How serious is it? Is this why you stopped using Skype? So I couldn't see you?'

She nodded her head softly.

Anita looked from Mahalia to Beau, and out the windows. She looked back at her sister again. She bit her lip. 'Cancer.'

'What treatment are you having?' Mahalia turned to Beau. 'We can help her, right? We can do whatever is needed?' The panic in her voice filled the room. Desperation screeched out, and she started shaking.

'Tell me you're going to get better; 'Nita, you're going to get better, right?'

'I've come home to die.' The words were spoken softly, but honestly.

An involuntary scream left Mahalia's mouth, and she fell to her sister's feet.

'No. No! You can't do this! Beau? Tell me there's something we can do. Medicine we can buy. Specialists we can hire. Tell me!'

Beau had never felt so powerless in his life, not even on his wedding night with Margaret Pilkington when he lay there impotent. The second he caught Anita's eyes at the airport, he knew that the prognosis wasn't good. The nurse confirmed his worst suspicions.

Beau wrapped his arms around both of them. Yes, he could buy any doctor or medicine that was on offer. Of course he could! There was no question of that. Yes, he'd do that. But how could he tell Mahalia that there are some things that money can't buy? That when the human body loses the fight to live only The Breathmaker decides who will live or die?

'Tell us everything Anita. How long have you got?'

'*How long has she got?* What sort of question is that?' Mahalia snapped.

Beau had never seen her so angry.

Mahalia was a good person; she didn't deserve what was about to happen, and from what he could see, Anita most certainly didn't either.

'Sweetheart, the only thing we can do is to make her comfortable.'

'I can't believe you're giving up. If it was your sister, you wouldn't just stand there and say: *make her comfortable.*' Mahalia paced the room. Beau didn't try to calm her. She needed to yell and move. It was her body's way of coping. Adrenaline needed movement, and he let her do what she had to in order to move the energy through her angry body.

'Beau's right. I've had everything that can possibly help, and it hasn't. It has delayed things, and they made me 'comfortable' so I could fly home, but now it's just a matter of time. I wanted to be home…with you, with Mom and Dad. Let me die in peace; and Hali, *you* need to make peace with this. I know it's hard. It took me a long time to come to terms with it. I was in denial for so long, even when my hair fell out. But I need you to be

131

with me, and I need you to let me go, too.'

'Do you know what you're even asking of me?' Mahalia cried.

Beau had quietly left the room, so they could continue their intimate conversation. Firstly, he checked the spare room was in order, and brought the bouquet from his room into it to brighten the place up a bit. His mind was racing. Where was the best place for her to be cared for? Red Maple Manor? Mahalia's Asheville apartment? A hospice? No, they'd all hate that. What about Jack's old house at Limetree Hollow? It would give the sisters some privacy, but be close enough to Beau in case they needed anything. He dismissed the idea. Selfish as it seemed, and as angry as Mahalia was with him, he didn't want to be apart from her. No, it was settled. They'd go back to Red Maple Manor, and their parents could stay there too.

Beau phoned Bessie, his maid, giving her umpteen instructions for food, flowers, bedding, and reading material. He then called his mate Jacob at the Anderson Cancer Centre in Houston. They'd met on holiday one year, and became firm friends. Jacob arranged to have three specialist cancer nurses fly up to North Carolina. He admitted to Beau that, at this point, the only care would be palliative. There'd be no recovery. Jacob offered to come up himself and give Anita a full check-over and a second opinion.

'I really appreciate that. I'll cover everyone's costs, and then some. I just need to know that I'm doing everything that can possibly be done. Anita's sister means the world to me, and I can't bear to see either of them suffering.'

Beau hung up the phone and put his head in

his hands in desperation, unaware that Mahalia was watching him from the doorway.

'I'm sorry,' she said softly.

Beau thought he was dreaming until she said it again.

'Beau, I'm so sorry. I overreacted, and I took it out on you. I'm so dreadfully ashamed of my behaviour.'

He looked up, tears in his eyes. 'You have nothing to apologise for. Ever. How's Anita doing?'

'She's sleeping on the sofa.'

'This room is ready for her, but it's best to just let her sleep where she is for now.'

'I heard you on the phone. Was that your friend Jacob you were talking to?'

'Yeah.'

'Thank you.'

They sat beside each other on the bed.

'Mom and Dad already know,' she said, still in shock. 'They've known for months, apparently. They flew out to Australia last month. I had no idea. They tried to convince her to come home then, but she was still thinking that she could fight it. They paid for her to come back, and for the nurses to fly with her.'

'Tell them they can stay at the Manor for as long as they like.'

'Really?'

'Of course. Honey, it's your home too.'

Anita settled into the guest room at Red Maple Manor, and was deeply appreciative of the stunning views. Jacob, and the small team of round-the-clock specialist nurses which accompanied him, arrived that afternoon. Jacob had marmalade hair, and a gentle soul.

'Beau, I gotta tell y'all, I don't know how she

managed that long-haul flight. It shows a real fightin' spirit. I don't know how she got permission to fly. But she's got a week left, at most. I hate to be the one to tell y'all. I've made her as comfortable as possible. The nurses know what they're doing. This is a time for goodbyes.'

'I appreciate your honesty,' Beau said, gulping down his exasperation.

'Hali, bury me next to granddad. Bring me flowers. Sing to me. Play me the guitar like you used to. Promise me, sis.'

Mahalia's tears fell, and try as she might to choke them back, she couldn't stop the crying. This was not the reunion she was meant to have with her kid sister.

'Don't leave me. You can't die.'

'If I could stay, I would. I came back to be with you, but that's all the fight I've got left in me.'

'But you're too young to die. You're too young! You're my sister. I need you.'

'Live for me, sis. Live for *me*.'

'Why didn't you tell me, damn it? Why did you leave it so bloody long?'

'Because you were happy. You sounded so deliriously happy that I just couldn't tell you. I didn't want to burst your bubble. You are so in love with Beau.'

'But you needed me. That should have come first!'

'I'm here now. Let's make the most of whatever time we have left. Please.'

And they did. Mahalia sat patiently by her side, day and night. She sang her songs, and from time to time when Beau would sing a few tunes too.

Lydia and Lester arrived early, and wrapped their arms around their crying daughters.

Beau showed them to their room, but they spent every moment of the next few days in with Mahalia and Anita. He arranged for some beds and bedding to be brought into the room so they could all be comfortable. Beau was doing everything humanly possible to give Mahalia's family what they needed, but the pain wasn't something he could fix.

'She's too young to die,' Mahalia cried into Beau's chest that night. 'She's too young. It's not fair. Damn it, it's not fair!'

'You're right, sweetheart, it's not fair,' he said as he held her. It felt as if they hadn't properly held each other in months, but in fact it was less than a week. Oh how quickly life can change direction.

Mahalia had a shower, and changed into jeans and a purple T-shirt. She hadn't changed in days, as she'd not wanted to leave her sister's side even while she was sleeping.

She headed to the kitchen, grateful that Bessie had been feeding them and fetching cups of tea. But today, she needed to cook. It was as if her hands had been tied up. Mahalia didn't know who she was when she wasn't cooking. First, she phoned the café. Everything was humming along beautifully, and she was truly grateful to have such a reliable and honest manager.

At first, she prepared a light salad, and some steamed vegetables with a lemon and black-pepper sauce, doubting that anyone upstairs had much of an appetite. Mahalia had needed this little bit of time to herself, so she could cry without upsetting her family even more than they were already. As she stood over the sink, gently sobbing, her tears trickled down the plughole. What started as gentle crying soon became convulsive howling.

'Honey, you need to come upstairs.' Beau's voice was solemn.

'Please tell me she hasn't gone?' Mahalia's voice was filled with panic.

'Not yet, but the nurses say it's nearly time.'

Mahalia abandoned the food. The banging of her heart continued as she took the stairs two at a time.

Lydia and Lester sat on one side of the bed, leaving space on the other side for Mahalia.

'Beau, come in with me,' she pleaded. 'I need you. I need you now more than ever.'

They sat, together, hand in hand; both of them shaking. Watching. Waiting for the last breath. The nurses stood reverently at the back of the room, like a trio of guardian angels. Respectfully, they allowed the family to say goodbye.

'I love you, Anita' Mahalia whispered to her baby sister one last time, holding her fragile hand as the final breath said *Enough now. I've had enough.* Despite the torment screaming through their hearts, they could all see a visible peace ease onto Anita's face. Truly resting now; no more pain.

'Sleep now, baby girl,' Mahalia cried. 'Sleep, sweet sister. I shall never ever forget you.'

Lydia and Lester sobbed into the sheets, their hands holding Anita's.

Mahalia would wrap her memories of Anita deep within her heart. Somehow she would hold her inside forever. But how would she live without Anita's middle-of-the-night phone calls and surprise packets in the post? Or the laughter that she always gave so willingly? Was that gone now? Forever? Just like that? The gaping hole inside would never be repaired. After all these years as best friends, she was gone. How was that possible?

That night brought them more than the loss of a beloved sister and daughter; it gifted them with the realisation that every moment of every day is priceless. Even after several hours, it felt impossible to stand up and leave the room. Anita may no longer have been in her body, but they could feel her soul hovering close by, offering them comfort in their time of greatest need. Even the nurses shed tears, despite facing this situation all through their working lives. They weren't immune to the beauty in Anita's death; and the love of her family, as she left this world, was something that they'd take back with them to each passing they were witness to, reminding them that what they did was more than a career: it was a calling.

Anita Rebecca Mason was buried in the churchyard, next to her grandfather. Beau had arranged most of the ceremony, leaving Mahalia and her parents to grieve and call their friends and other family.

Her body, wrapped simply in a cloth shroud and draped in native wildflowers, was laid to rest alongside the man who had been so generous to her, and had given her the financial wings to travel to Australia and live there.

Beau called Lola and Russ to sing hymns. It was a fitting tribute to a woman raised on Bluegrass music. They sang *A Beautiful Life*, and *The Church in the Wildwood*.

Afterwards, the mourners gathered at Red Maple Manor. Mahalia was touched that Anita's friends had come from near and far, some from Australia. Their willingness to travel such a distance for a one-hour ceremony was a testament to the impact Anita had on the lives of everyone who knew her. The wake gave Mahalia a chance to get to know her sister better, and despite her heart being ripped in two, she couldn't help but smile and laugh at some of the stories that she heard. *Oh yes, that's Anita*, she said more than once.

The Shadow of Grief

Every day, Mahalia would ride her horse over to the church house, a bunch of wildflowers in her hands, and sing Anita's favourite song: *Sunshine on my Shoulders*.

They were the darkest days of her life. Heavy days. Lost in grief, it was as if part of her body had been cut off, and her heart surgically removed. Unlike anything she'd ever experienced in her life, more than once she wondered if she'd ever feel normal again. The pain touched her at the deepest cellular level, transforming her in ways she didn't know were possible. She questioned everything, including her faith. What sort of God would do something so callous? No God she'd ever been taught to love and believe in, that's for sure. Without her faith, who was she?

Beau felt like he was losing her. Even when he looked into her eyes, he couldn't reach her. The haunting emptiness terrified him. With each passing day, she avoided his hugs. Every platonic advance was rejected. Didn't she need him anymore? Beau's greatest fears came to the surface: that something would tear their relationship apart. All this time he'd worried about how Margaret could destroy them with her lies and manipulation, and now it was being eroded by someone that Mahalia loved deeply: her sister. It was a cruel irony.

Mahalia started sleeping in the guest room. *Needed space*, she had said.

'I just want to be on my own, and not think about anyone else. I don't want to talk to anyone. I need to grieve, and I can't do that around other people.'

Beau honoured the dark place she inhabited, and agreed she could sleep in the other room and hoped it was just her way of trying to feel close to Anita: by sleeping in the same bed that she had.

One thing Beau wasn't going to do was push Mahalia back into his bed. But he was at a complete loss as to how to comfort her, protect her, love her. Each day he picked wildflowers for her, and quietly placed them in her bedroom. He'd fetch cups of tea, and run a hot bath each evening. Few words were spoken, but he ensured that she was always aware of his presence, of his kindnesses. Not once did he go any further than the boundaries of the property, but relied on his housekeeper for any errands.

It was a Sunday morning, five long and drawn-out weeks later, when he was startled to find Mahalia driving down the road in her pick-up truck leaving nothing but a trail of dust. No note. No goodbye. Beau sighed with relief to see her turn right towards her grandfather's old house.

Beau followed her down there and then walked to where she was kneeling on the grass.

The church bells chimed in the distance, reminding them both of who lay in the churchyard cemetery. Everything that needed to be said was expressed when they searched each other's eyes.

'Honey, what are you doing?' he asked as he sat down beside her in the side garden near the vegetable beds.

'Pottering,' she smiled weakly. 'Just pottering. I thought I'd get a start on making this place ready for teaching classes. Kathryn's under pressure from her boss for me to do another three photographs, and I figured it might be better to get this place in order first and then I can get into it.'

'Are you ready for that? These are such early days in your grieving. I'm sure the publisher would understand that.'

'Anita would want me to. She'd be furious that I've been so miserable.'

Beau nodded. 'Right then, what do you need for this place?' He recognised that he might not have been any good to her emotionally, but he could at least be supportive on a practical level.

'Truthfully? I need my plants from the balcony,' and her face grimaced. 'Hestia and Ellie have been watering them, but it's a huge job to bring them out here.'

'Don't worry, I know just the man for the job. What else do you need?'

Mahalia gave him a list, and he mentally compiled it into a to-do-in-order-of-priority list.

'I've missed you,' she said, taking a few steps closer. 'I've really missed you! It feels like we've been on opposite ends of the planet.'

Beau leaned forward and kissed her on her forehead.

'God I've missed you too. I thought I'd lost you. I really had.'

'That could never happen. I'm never leaving you, Beau. No matter what. I'm not going to break that promise. You can't get rid of me that easily,' she smiled.

'Well that's a relief.'

And within about forty seconds they were inside the house, on a bare mattress, doing what they did best.

Mahalia cried while they made love, but she didn't want to stop. Beau's arms around her, and to feel him deep inside, were all that she needed. The huge hole in her heart needing filling, and she felt his love, comfort, and promise of a solid future. Every movement was a reminder that they were alive, and had a whole lot of living to do. And there were tears because Anita would never make love again, and because she, Mahalia Mason, had a whole lifetime of loving to look forward to: every single day. And it was the most glorious sort of loving. Beau was a man who treasured her, and wanted only the best. Every day he treated her like a queen, and she honoured him as if he were the king. More tears were shed as she cried at the thought of Beau dying, and how she'd never be able to stand up again if he wasn't in her life. Beau held her tenderly while she sobbed her heart out. 'Don't let go of me,' she pleaded.

They made love gently, and reverently. There was a time for hot, passionate, steamy, heart-pounding sex, and there were times for lovemaking so gentle that it consumed every part of one's soul and made the angels sing. Today was one of those days.

'I love you, Mahalia,' he whispered.

'I know you do, honey. I know. I'm sorry I've been so distant. It just hurts so much knowing I'll never see Anita again, or hear her laughter. It hurts!'

There were no words to ease her pain. Instead, he held her close. If that's all he could ever do to be a healing balm, then he'd do that day and night.

The next afternoon Keith McVeigh drove down the road in Mahalia's pick-up truck, heaving with potted plants.

'So you were the hired help,' she said sarcastically.

'I'm sorry about what happened,' he said.

What had Beau said and done to make this man so repentant?

'If there's ever a next time, I won't miss with the pitch fork,' she promised.

They both grinned, and she knew in that moment that she'd always be safe here at Limetree Hollow. Whatever Beau Candler had said, or done, to Keith, one thing was for sure: his lecherous days were over!

Mahalia carried bags, trays and pots around the garden, and marked out where she'd plant everything. In her heart, she felt herself come alive. There *was* life after death.

It was easy to photograph here, and she loved how the afternoon light brought an ambience to the various settings she conjured.

Long after the final photos were submitted to HarperCollins, Mahalia continued to photograph at Limetree Hollow. Fall brought mustard and scarlet leaves to the mountain side, and mists shrouded the wooden homestead. It was a time of letting go. Although Mahalia was still raw with pain, she had moved to a new place in her grief; there was a shift inside her, just like the changing seasons. Autumnal sunshine brought breathtaking light, and the radiant foliage made her smile. That she could laugh at the antics of a rabbit in the vegetable patch gave her hope. She felt something growing inside her heart, she wasn't sure what, but with it came the certain knowledge that if she ever gave birth to a daughter, her name would be Hope. Without hope, there'd be no point living.

Laughter had been slow to return. Every day, every moment, felt like wading through shoulder-high treacle. So often she wondered if she'd ever get her life back. In many ways, the life she was living and planning before Anita died somehow seemed irrelevant. Ambition and dreams seemed pointless, somehow. What was the point of anything if we were just going to die?

Lester and Lydia came down to stay at the homestead, every so often. It was their way of being close to their only living daughter, but without invading her privacy at the manor.

The loss had torn the family apart, and was bringing the remaining three back together. No longer a quartet, but a trio. Their music was different now; haunting, melancholic, but still sweet and beautiful in the way only a truly loving family can be. Mahalia prepared picnics for sharing on the verandah, and under the cedar trees. They walked up the ridge, and they all helped stack firewood for the Winter ahead. Soon the snow would fall, and travel wouldn't be so easy.

Mahalia's parents said their goodbyes, and promised they'd be back when the weather improved. It felt like another death every time they said goodbye, but there was talk of them selling up and moving back to North Carolina. Just those words were like comfort food after a long illness, and Mahalia shed tears at their promises.

Delicious

The first snow storm of the season whipped up violent howling winds, and tumbled a courier delivery up the driveway right to the front doors of Red Maple Manor.

'Are you expecting something, honey?' Mahalia asked Beau. He looked up from his coffee. 'No. Surprised they got up the driveway.'

Mahalia met the driver at the front door, eager to grab the package, but not so eager to let in the flying snowflakes.

'Ms Mason?'

'Yes,' she said, shivering in the cold wind.

'Delivery for you.'

When she took hold of it, she said 'Fancy a coffee? It's so cold out there!'

'Love one,' he followed her into the kitchen and joined them for morning tea.

'Oh my God, it's my book!' she said as she opened it.

Mahalia waved it around the kitchen, dancing with delight, her fingers trembling at the prized possession.

'Show me,' Beau beckoned.

'*Gifts From My Cookfire*,' he said. 'Great title. Wow, look at those photos! This is so much more than a recipe book.' Tears came to his eyes when he saw the dedication.

```
       For the love of my life, Beau.

And in memory of my beautiful sister, Anita.
   Living life for you every single day,
               sweetheart.
```

'I didn't think I'd see a copy till the launch next week. This is so exciting. Kathryn's done a great job.'

'*You* did a great job. Don't give the credit to someone else.'

The launch of *Gifts From My Cookfire* was to be held in New York's legendary Strand Bookshop, on Broadway. Mahalia had been there many times before, and it was always her preferred habitat when in New York. There was history to the place, even down to it being named after the famous street in London where writers and publishers expanded their works.

Mahalia thrived on the smell of paper: new books, old books; and the excitement of so many people hunting for just the right one. The whole place was utterly disorganised, big, and dusty; and it was survival of the fittest when searching for a book. But she could think of no place more perfect than here for launching her book into the world. Although the event was being catered, she couldn't help bring along samples from her book. If nothing else, it would make the publication come alive for people to smell, taste and see her meals.

In many ways, despite being a successful business woman, Mahalia did most of her work behind the scenes: pottering away in the kitchen creating recipes. Standing in front of so many people, describing her recipe choices, and how she photographed the meals, and where her inspiration came from, she was struck by how daunting it must be to do author tours on a full-time basis. She was surprised by how nervous she felt.

Mahalia shared her love and passion for good food, and how she learnt to cook not from her mother—who was actually a fine cook—but from her late grandfather,

Jack, a man who willingly gave her free rein in his kitchen from the age of five. She shared photos of his homestead, and the herb gardens, and of the verandah where they sat and ate meals all Summer long. More than once, she had to dab her eyes when nostalgia overwhelmed her.

'My grandfather didn't actually teach me how to cook, as such, but gave me the freedom to be creative. More than once he ate pancakes that not even a dog would wolf down, but he always encouraged me rather than criticised. I love him for that.'

Afterwards, she breathed a sigh of relief that this was a one-off event, and that the only place she was going to was Red Maple Manor.

There was appreciation for the long hours people spent in line waiting for a moment with her; she spent more time than she ever expected on signing books. Beau waited patiently, and more than once headed off to the music section.

'I think you've bought more books than I've sold,' she laughed.

'Just essential supplies,' he laughed. 'Found a few you might like, too.'

The owners thanked her profusely for giving up her time, and her editor, Kathryn, was absolutely delighted by the turnout.

'Have you given any more thought to the TV series? We really need an answer now,' Kathryn asked.

'What TV series?' Beau asked, surprised by the news.

Kathryn replied, 'It would be a tie-in with the book and café. Mahalia, I can't believe you haven't told Superman!'

Beau chuckled at this permanent nickname the women had developed.

'Well, are you interested?' Kathryn asked casually, trying not to sound desperate. Her bosses were on her case to get an answer as soon as possible. 'We'd film in the café in the evenings so it didn't interfere with normal opening hours. I'll call you in two days. You look like you need a good night's sleep! But I need an answer.'

'What do you think about the TV offer?' Beau asked her the next day when they drove into the lane of Red Maple Manor. 'And why didn't you tell me? This is a huge opportunity.'

'I haven't given it too much thought. It would be amazing for the café, but... I have to admit that it's exciting, but I like my privacy. I'd lose that instantly. I'm not ready to give that up. I don't want to give that up. Maybe it's selfish, but I have everything I need. I have *you*. I don't want anything else.'

'So long as you're sure about that,' he said as they pulled up in front of the manor.

Kathryn phoned first thing the next morning.

'What are your thoughts on the TV show? It would be brilliant for your career!'

'My career is just fine, Kathryn,' Mahalia laughed.

'Perhaps we should meet up and talk about it some more?' Kathryn offered. When there was no answer, she added 'Why don't I meet you in the café. I can introduce you to Joshua, the producer who would be in charge of it all.'

'You've already got a producer in mind?' Mahalia

asked, absolutely shocked at the speed at which things were happening. 'I haven't even agreed yet.'

'Tomorrow at 5pm?' Kathryn would tease the answer out of her one way or another.

'Sure, I'll meet you at five!'

'Honey, am I making a mistake by saying no?' she asked Beau the next morning as they lazed in bed, their legs tangled around each other.

'Only you can answer this. What is your biggest fear about saying yes? Is it really just about losing your anonymity or is it a fear of being successful?'

'What do you mean?' she asked, more than a little confused.

'At the moment, you feel in control of everything in your life. You choose your work hours, you choose your staff, you choose everything. If you take on this TV series, some of that will change. Perhaps a lot of it will change. You'll be working for someone else, for a start. And if it becomes really successful, you won't be just another face on the street. Everyone will want a part of you. That sort of success can be intimidating.'

'Wow, well that's just helped my resolve. Thanks!' she laughed.

'However,' he said, keen to show her the other side, 'we live in a culture which lives off junk food, and most people have no sense of what real food tastes like, and how nutritious your style of eating is. This TV show could change lives. You could, singlehandedly, inspire a whole generation of teenagers into the kitchen. There's a lot of power to be had while you're ripping up basil leaves and toasting sunflower seeds! You really shouldn't dismiss the idea too quickly.'

'Well when you put it that way, what choice do I

have?' she asked. 'You make it sound like it would be selfish of me to decline.'

'I never said that, exactly...' and he pulled her into his arms. 'Whatever choice you make will be the right one. This is your life. You have to live with the consequences.'

Kathryn and Joshua were seated in the Citrus Avenue Café when Mahalia arrived. The doors were closed to customers, and Hestia was just tidying up for the day.

'I'll leave you to it,' she said when Mahalia came in the door.

'Thanks for everything, Hestia. The place is looking fabulous.' She pecked her on the cheek, and walked over to where Kathryn and Joshua were enjoying lattes.

'Hi Mahalia, I'm Joshua,' the young man said as he stood up. 'So excited at the possibilities here. The café is amazing, really. It's unlike any I've ever been in. And the recipes in your book, and the photos...well, wow. It's a winning combination.'

If she wasn't so madly in love with Beau, she'd probably fall for Joshua's twinkling blue eyes, messy blond hair, and vibrant energy. There was an immediate connection between them, but she filed it away as nothing more than creative chemistry.

'I have to admit that it all sounds exciting, but I'm really nervous.'

'Don't be. I have a great team behind me, and we'll minimise any disruption to the normal running of the café. Everything will be tidied up after each shoot, and we'll make things as seamless as possible.'

'You make it sound too easy, and *that* makes me nervous too,' she laughed.

Kathryn was completely oblivious to the fact that

Joshua had just fallen head over heels for Mahalia. If she'd sensed it, then she'd probably put a stop to it herself. After all, she knew everything that Mahalia and Beau had been through, and she wasn't about to let anything get in the way of that. Mahalia was her talent, and she was protective of her well-being.

'If I say yes, when would we start?' she asked.

Joshua's face lit up. 'My team is ready to roll. We just need your permission; and some forms to sign. We could start filming within days. What do you say? Are you game?'

How could she resist his charms? He was so passionate about what she had to offer.

'That soon? Okay, I'll do it,' she laughed, relieved that she'd finally made a decision.

Joshua jumped to his feet and wrapped his arms around her. Oh yes, he had fallen.

'Right, we want as much prepublicity as possible,' he said, settling down to business again. 'Megan, our PR girl, will be in touch and organise various media interviews.'

'This sounds hectic already,' Mahalia said, taking in a deep breath.

'Features in the New York Times, Boston Globe, Boston Herald, The Charlotte Observer, and so on, plus radio interviews. It'll be intense for while, but it'll make all the difference to the show. We'll film six shows to start with, but there's no doubt that we'll get commissioned for several six-parters.'

The next few weeks were intense, as Mahalia spent each evening at the café filming the first two shows. Despite the exhausting schedule, she enjoyed it. Joshua was incredibly creative and talented, and his enthusiasm rubbed off on her and the whole crew.

Mahalia felt fully supported by Beau, and he accompanied her to interviews, bringing in hairdressers and stylists before photo shoots. The aim of the publicity department was to generate a lot of interest before the first show went to air, and really excite the imagination of the public.

It was only when they were driving through Asheville to dinner one night that Mahalia began to get an inkling of the full impact that being in the spotlight was going to have. They turned into Lexington Avenue. They were driving to the New York Times-recommended Indian restaurant, *Mela*.

'Oh no!' she cried out, when it first caught her eye. The billboard was 12 metres by 8 metres, and her face was smiling down at her. Those fiery copper curls seemed larger than life.

'Oh yes!' Beau laughed. 'You look fantastic.'

'I don't exactly want to see my face when I'm going through town, though.'

'But it's such a beautiful face,' Beau said. 'That is an amazing photograph, Mahalia. You should be proud of it, especially given your eye for photography.'

And then a bus went by with the same poster telling everyone in town that their very own Asheville treasure was going to be on US TV sharing the best of her recipes.

'This feels overwhelming,' she confided. 'It's not like I'm someone who can blend into the crowd. Not with this hair!'

'You'll get used to it.'

'I think I need more time before this all goes to air. I was looking forward to it, in a strange sort of way…'

'None of that has to change. Just take one day at a time. Look at the details rather than the bigger picture.'

'Even *that* big picture!' she said, pointing up at herself. They both started laughing.

They stepped into what was known as the best Indian restaurant in Western North Carolina.

'It probably won't be as good as your Indian food,' Beau said.

'Oh it's good, I promise you. I've eaten here many times. It's not just the food that's great, the chefs are wonderful, and they're certified by the Appalachian Sustainable Agriculture Project for using ingredients produced by local farmers. Things like that win me over every time,' Mahalia said. She was passionate about local, organic and sustainable produce.

The waiter led them to their reserved table, and already she could feel eyes on her.

'Tell me I'm not imagining it,' she whispered to Beau.

'People recognise you. Just smile and be gracious. At least you're in your hometown, and the response is friendly.'

They began looking through the menu, when Mahalia heard her name called.

'Joshua? Hi, what are you doing here?'

'I've come to sample some more of Asheville. I want to make the most of being in this part of the world.'

'This is Beau, my partner,' she said, introducing the two men to each other.

'Are you dining alone?' Beau asked.

'Just grabbing a takeaway, actually,' Joshua replied.

'You're welcome to join us, if you like,' Beau offered.

'Really? That'd be great. Thanks so much!'

Conversation was largely based around the TV show, and Joshua's plans and ideas. Beau couldn't help notice how Joshua's eyes rarely left Mahalia, and he felt annoyed at himself that jealousy was rearing its head. Of course he had nothing to worry about. Mahalia was just being her friendly self. Of course she wouldn't think about being with Joshua. But still, something nagged at Beau. He couldn't quite put his finger on it. And who was he to put a dampener on the evening? *He* had encouraged Mahalia to do the show. *He* had invited Joshua to join them.

They shared a hearty buffet of Indian lentil wafers, served with mint-cilantro chutney. After a glass of fine wine, it was followed by strips of fresh paneer cheese dipped in a mildly spiced-chickpea batter, and then deep fried. They nibbled on Naan bread, filled with nuts, dried fruit and raisins, while they awaited their main meals.

Mahalia chose her favourites for them to share: Tandoor-roasted eggplant, mashed, seasoned and sautéed with onions and tomatoes; delicately spiced chickpeas in a tomato base with cilantro, paprika and chilli; fresh okra in a spicy sauce of onions, and cumin seeds.

Joshua chose ground almonds, cashews and paneer cheese formed into balls and cooked in a rich almond-spice sauce, and Beau contributed to their buffet by ordering vegetables cooked in a hot and spicy Goan sauce.

Beau was conflicted. He liked Joshua, and could see he was passionate about his job, but he wasn't keen on that same passion extending towards Mahalia.

'You sure look incredible on the billboards,' Joshua said to her, leaning in close. Far too close.

'Thanks. It all feels rather surreal.' When she looked at Beau, and smiled, he reached over and held her hands.

'I couldn't do any of this without Beau by my side.'

Joshua reached for his wine. 'Really great getting to know you Beau, but I best be on my way. Busy week coming up. Thanks for a great evening. You've got a fabulous woman there!'

'Nice guy, isn't he?' Mahalia said as she watched him walk away.

'He's got the hots for you Mahalia. Be careful.'

'What are you talking about?' she laughed. 'Of course he doesn't!'

'Even a blind man could see it.' Beau said, crumpling his linen napkin into the centre of the empty plate.

'Really? You think he likes me in that way? Well, I think he's a wonderful person to work with. He's clever, funny, creative...'

'I get the idea honey. I'm glad he's all those things, and more. It's the *more* I want you to be careful of, okay?'

'Do you really think I'd ever look at another man again?' she asked, seriously.

'Maybe not deliberately. Sometimes these things just sneak up on us and catch us unaware. You're going to be spending a hell of a lot of time together in the next few months. It's only reasonable that you'd become quite intimate, emotionally.'

'Beau, don't say another word. Please. I like him. I really like him. But I like him as a friend, like a brother or a cousin. I don't see him as a lover. I only have eyes for you. Now put that jealousy away. I can't bear it. If you can't trust me, then what hope is there for us?'

'I do trust you. I really do. It's that, well, what healthy man wouldn't want to be with you? What man wouldn't want to be your lover?'

'I'm finding this conversation very distressing. Do you think we could end it now?'

'Of course. I'm sorry honey. Shall we go home now?'

'Sure.'

On the drive back to Red Maple Manor, her mind was ticking over. What if Beau was right? What if things changed between her and Joshua? What if her feelings developed into something she couldn't control? And what would happen if all the love and passion she felt for Beau was transferred to Joshua? She shuddered at the encroaching thoughts.

'I'll pull out of the contract if you want.'

'Honey, I don't want that. I'm thrilled you're doing this show. I just didn't give a thought to how it would bring people into your life that might prove to be...'

'Competition?'

He sighed deeply, somewhat embarrassed.

'Yes.'

'Come to every filming session if you want. Chaperone me twenty-four seven if it makes you feel secure. Do whatever you need to do to feel safe in the knowledge that you're the only man for me, Beau. Now, and forever.'

'I'm sorry. Maybe it was the wine speaking.'

'You only had one glass! It wasn't wine speaking; it was your inner tribal man!' Mahalia held back her laugh; she didn't want to give him the satisfaction that part of her actually found it somewhat funny.

They'd finished brushing their teeth, and were preparing for bed. Beau lifted her up onto the bathroom basin counter and kissed her. He'd hoped they'd make love tonight, and that it might soothe their recent conversation, but he wasn't expecting this explosion of passion here in the bathroom. It spoke a thousand words for how he felt: He wanted to be the only man she thought of tonight, not Joshua.

'You need to know that you're the only man for me, but I don't know how to prove it to you. I live with you. My whole life is oriented towards you. I give my body wholeheartedly and willingly to you. I share all my deepest thoughts. I don't know what else I can do. I'm at a loss here, Beau. Help me out, please.'

As much as he wanted to be inside her, for now he'd give her what she needed most from him: *time, patience, respect.* Slowly, he opened her like a flower, unfurling one petal at a time.

Incessant, overlapping moans of pleasure and delight gave way to a deep earthy groan, a whole octave lower, as she reached for the Moon and called out his name across the night.

Cinder

Before she left for more filming in Asheville, Mahalia had to clear up the tension she felt about Beau's jealousy. In her heart, she had to find some resolution before committing herself to spending such long hours working side by side with Joshua.

'Why are you so jealous? I mean, it's clear that if it wasn't Josh it would be someone else. What reason have I ever given you to be jealous?' Her words were calm, not accusatory. 'I need to know, Beau. I want to understand you, and I want to avoid any incendiary situations. Has someone cheated on you? Did some woman break your heart?'

There was no getting around the issue. Beau could see that she wanted an answer, and he had no choice but to be honest for she'd see through any white lies.

'No, it's nothing to do with any other woman. It's you. It's always about you. You're amazing. Everything about you makes me want to hold on tighter, and I never want to let you go. It's not just physical, it's everything. The way you listen, and hear me. Your laughter, and your touch. That way you kiss me, or giggle into my shoulder. To me, you're perfect. I've...' Beau rushed his hands through his hair. There was nothing worse than wearing your heart on your sleeve. 'I've never been so scared of losing anything in my life. I'm ashamed to say this Mahalia, but...I can buy pretty well anything I want in this world. And with that, comes a sense of power. But you? I can't buy you. I can't own you. I can't control you. Not that I want to have that sort of power over you. I don't. I really don't. But sometimes when I'm with you, and there's a man nearby, I feel completely impotent. I can't stand it! I want you to be with me because you want to be. Of all the men in this world, you're with me. I'm terrified you're going to wake up and see how big this world is and how many choices there are.'

That was that. That was the truth. She could make of it what she wanted.

It was her turn to speak now.

'When you look far into the future, do you see me there?' she asked

'Yes. Of course I do. I only see you.'

'Then just keep seeing into the future because you're the only one I see there. I'm not looking for anyone else. My love for you is complete, it's all-consuming. You stole my heart eight years ago, Beau. No one else ever had a chance after I saw you. That's the truth. That's *my* truth.'

Mahalia wrapped her arms around him. 'I love you Beau. I've always loved you.'

It was 4pm, and filming would begin in an hour. Mahalia ushered the staff from the café, and began her preparations. It was important for her to feel ahead of the film crew, and mentally on top of the meal she was preparing.

She'd only been at work for ten minutes when Joshua showed up. Early!

'Joshua, hi. I wasn't expecting you until five.'

'Hey Mahalia, I was already in the area, so thought I'd pop by on the chance you were in.'

In his typically enthusiastic style, he started sharing his ideas for camera shots, and close ups. Mahalia did her best to let Beau's words evaporate. There was no room here for any of his alpha-male inclinations. She had a job to do. While Joshua was scribbling down notes, she studied him and then realised that it was no surprise Beau was jealous. Joshua was pretty cute! And with that, she put those traitorous thoughts to one side, and listened intently.

Filming had turned out to be quite fun, despite her initial hesitation.

Joshua thought she was a natural, and she spoke to the camera with the same joy and enthusiasm as she would to her best friend.

More than once, he told her that he loved the way she handled vegetables; though he was caught off guard by her expertise when slicing a cucumber. The film crew felt their tummies rumble, and found it hard to concentrate on the job at hand when they were surrounded by so many exotic and tempting aromas. A perk to the job was getting to sample Mahalia's creations.

For the next three weeks, they filmed every night of the week. The schedule was hectic and exhausting, but deeply exhilarating. Every other night was spent in Asheville to avoid the daily commute to Red Maple Manor. It was late on Friday night, and the film crew had gone home; Mahalia and Joshua were the only two people left at the Citrus Avenue Café. The lights were dim, so as not to attract the attention of people strolling by.

'The feedback from the media interviews has been incredible. People are really excited about this,' Joshua said when they sat back and dined on grilled eggplants stuffed with ricotta, sultanas and Middle Eastern spices. 'This food is amazing!'

'Thank you. The interviews were quite fun, actually. Most of them!'

'We'll probably wrap up filming next week. We've got enough to work with already, but I prefer to have too much footage than just enough. Do you think you can manage another week?' he asked kindly.

But she didn't answer. Beau was at the door. She jumped up from her seat, unlocked the door, and rushed to his arms.

'Darling, what a lovely surprise! I'm so glad you're here. We're just eating the food I made during filming. There's plenty if you want some.'

'Sounds great!' he said.

Mahalia was disarmed by his relaxed attitude. One look at them dining by candlelight was surely enough to arouse his suspicions, but he seemed calm and at ease.

'Hi Joshua, how's the filming?' Beau asked, shaking his hand firmly.

'Everything's on schedule. Footage is great. The talent is easy to work with, which makes a huge change. I can't tell you how frustrating it is to work with a diva. Mahalia's been a joy to be with every single day.'

'The phone hasn't stopped ringing. That piece in the Times is probably the best advertising you could have hoped for,' Beau said, feeling rather proud of Mahalia.

Feeling more relaxed that he was being friendly and charming towards Joshua, she kissed Beau on the cheek.

They stayed till midnight, and then said their goodbyes.

Mahalia was surprised by how happy she felt. Despite the grief still tormenting her heart, she had found satisfaction in taking part in filming, and in how successful the book was already proving to be: on the Top Ten bookseller charts.

No matter how heavy her heart felt from the loss of losing her only sister, she still had so very much to be grateful for. Life was good. She was deeply in love with Beau.

Beau and Mahalia sat upright in bed, shocked and dazed by the phone ringing in the hallway. One look at the bedside clock showing 3am meant it was either a wrong number or an emergency. The only person who ever phoned at this time was Anita, but she was gone now. Mahalia's heart somersaulted. Anita was gone. It wasn't Anita. She cried out in pain.

Beau bounded out of bed and answered it, hoping like hell that it wasn't Margaret.

'Beau Candler,' he answered firmly.

He listened quietly, and said, 'Just one minute.'

He walked back into the bedroom. 'It's for you.'

'Me?'

She hauled her achingly tired body out of bed. 'Hello, Mahalia Mason speaking.' As she listened, she sank to the floor, unable to speak for a few moments. 'Are you sure? I'll be there as quick as I can.'

'Honey, what is it?' Beau asked, concerned by her body language.

'Get dressed, I'll tell you in the car,' she cried. 'Take the Jeep not the Jag!'

Mahalia had never dressed so quickly in her life. Jeans, long-sleeved T-shirt, jumper, boots. She brushed her hair up into a ponytail and raced to the car. 'Hurry up, Beau!' Her hands were shaking.

They buckled their seatbelts, and he sped down the road. 'Where am I going?' he asked.

'The café. Or…' and she started crying, sobbing. 'What's left of the café!'

'What are you talking about? What's happened?'

'It's on fire.'

For most of the hour-long drive down the mountain, she kept her teary eyes firmly on the night lights of Asheville ahead of them.

'I don't understand how this can happen. I've got the latest fire and smoke detectors installed, and various alarms. I run regular staff training days on these things.'

'No building is fireproof, honey.'

'Yes, but…never mind.'

Mahalia caught her faulty breath as they entered the street to the sight of red lights flashing, and sirens blaring. The staccato lights left her feeling queasy and she wanted to close her eyes. There were easily a dozen firemen battling the blaze. 'Oh my God, there's nothing left.'

Beau pulled up at the end of the street, and held her in his arms.

'You'll get through this. We'll find a way to rebuild.'

'But it's my *baby*! It's not just a building. This is my life. I put everything I have into this: my heart, my soul, my love,' she sobbed.

'I know. I know.'

They stared in disbelief at the sight before them. It seemed impossible that just a handful of hours ago they had been sitting inside, laughing.

After a minute, Beau led her to the firefighters, looking for someone to speak to.

'Our inspectors need a few hours before they can get in there and find out what caused this. I'm so sorry for your loss Ms Mason. I hope you've got insurance,' the middle-aged chief said.

'Of course I've got insurance, but that's not the point. I have six full-time members of staff without jobs now! And I'm supposed to be filming here!'

'There's not much you can do here now. Like I say, we need a few hours for things to cool down. Come back at 8am, and we'll have a better sense of where things are at.'

They turned away, shocked, and simply held each other.

'Let's go back to your apartment,' Beau said.

'We can't. One of my staff members moved in yesterday.'

'Oh. Why didn't you tell me?'

'A lot on my mind, I suppose. Sorry.'

Beau held her close. There was nothing he could do to bring an end to the devastating scene before them. Hadn't she endured enough loss this year?

Even the outdoor citrus trees had become charred remains. There was nothing familiar to her as she looked at the sight: black charcoal, smoke, soot. If nothing else, she was grateful that the firefighters came soon enough to save the neighbouring buildings.

They walked the street, and headed up another two blocks to the all-night Pancake Parlour. 'May as well have breakfast, and sustain ourselves before the day ahead,' he said, leading her towards the front counter.

'Thick and fluffy pancake with scrambled eggs, grilled tomatoes and mushrooms, thanks,' she said, barely conscious of placing the order.

'Crepes, with just maple syrup on mine. Thanks.' Beau guided her to a small table in the corner.

They ate in silence, and at 7.30am Mahalia started making calls. First, to her café manager, then the remaining staff. 'I'll call you later and talk about pay,' she promised each and every one of them.

Then she phoned Joshua. He was desperate to come over and see her. Mahalia thought better of it. 'I'm fine. Beau and I will see the fire chief in a few minutes. I'll call you later. We can do the rest of the filming at our house, if you like…or I've got an old farmhouse we can film in if necessary.' She said goodbye, then walked hand in hand with Beau to the remains of the café.

Beau was desperate to make everything right for her. There were so many things in life that money could fix up, but this wasn't one of them. Mahalia was right. The café, and everything about it, was her baby. No amount of financial investment could compare to what she had invested emotionally into Citrus Avenue Café.

'Ma'am, we're trying to establish the owner of a Rolls Royce that was parked over the road by the butcher's shop just before the blaze began. Witnesses say it had a baby seat in it. That's all we've got to go on, as the number plates were covered. I've got to ask you. Do you have any enemies?' a policeman asked.

'Enemies?' Beau was furious. 'Does she look like the kind of woman who has enemies?'

The chief fire inspector was firm.

'With due respect, Ms Mason has had a lot of media coverage this past month. Anyone from her past could think of this as a perfect way to avenge themselves.'

'I don't have enemies. None that I know of,' she said weakly. 'You think this was started deliberately?' she asked, feeling sick to her bones. 'You think that the person who did this had a child?' She looked at Beau. No, surely not.

'Is there something I should know?' the chief asked.

'No. No. I need to go home. This is all too much for me. Can you call me and update when you get the chance?' she asked.

'Of course I can Ms Mason. In the meantime, if you have *any* idea who might do something like this, please let me know. This fire was no accident. Someone wanted the place burnt flat to the ground, and sadly, they got what they wanted. So, if there's *anything* you can tell me,' he looked her firmly in the eye, 'that would help us apprehend this person, I want to know.'

The ride back to Red Maple Manor was done in complete silence. They were both thinking the same thing: *Margaret*. Beau kept pushing the thought out of his mind. Yes, she'd done crazy things in her time, but a fire? It was incomprehensible that she'd go that far. Of course she didn't want Mahalia around, but to burn her café to the ground? Beau kept shaking his head in disbelief. No, it was one step too far.

When they got home, he opened the door of the car and led Mahalia inside. Without saying a word, she headed upstairs, silently fuming. The stench of the acrid fumes on her clothes and skin, and up her nostrils was unbearable. After taking a long shower, she sank into bed, wanting to hide from the world.

Beau joined her, but remained silent. When he reached out to hold her, she was non-responsive, so he turned the other way. Beau didn't want to admit that it was Margaret, but he didn't know what else to say. Instead of turning to each other, they turned away, and neither of them had ever felt more lonely in their lives.

At midday, Beau came back into the kitchen. Not for even a second did she look up from the cheese ploughman sandwiches she was preparing for their lunch.

Beau finally broke the silence.

'I know Margaret's crazy, but really, Mahalia, you don't honestly think she'd set your café on fire?'

'Are you so blind, Beau? Of course she did! I don't have enemies! A baby seat? It's just too coincidental for my liking. And…she owns a Rolls Royce as well as her BMW. You told me yourself.' And then she bit her tongue. Mahalia didn't want to say anything she might regret.

'And what?' Beau drew close to her, and placed a hand on each of her arms. 'And what, Mahalia? I know you want to say something else, so just say it. For God's sake, get it out of your system. I can see it's eating you up.'

'If you'd just had her put away in the first place… years ago, when she really needed psychological help, then we wouldn't have spent the past year trying to deal with your demons!' She could have kicked herself. It was a cruel thing to say, and she could tell by the way he winced, and pulled back from her, that she'd fired the arrow exactly where it needed to go.

And with those words, he slowly walked out of the room counting to ten. Beau was furious. Furious, because she was right. And then he turned around.

'Do you think your burnt-down café is my fault? Tell me. Tell me now what you really think?'

'Don't be ridiculous! I never said that. Of course it's not *your* fault. You didn't set it on fire! You didn't light the match. But...'

'But I'm partially to blame because she still walks the streets?'

'I'm not pointing the finger at you, Beau; I'm just saying this could have been avoided!'

Beau slammed the front door behind him, got into the Jaguar, and drove down the road.

Mahalia was beside herself with worry. It was important to be honest, but she hadn't meant to upset him.

Where was he going? What was he doing?

Surely he must understand how devastated she was to lose the café in this way? It was bad enough that she was still grieving deeply for her sister, but to have this loss on top of that was just too much to take.

For several hours she tried contacting him on his cellphone, but it kept going to voice mail. 'Damn it, Beau!' she said, more than once. 'You know it's the truth. Just admit it!'

A few hours later, the ringing doorbell had Mahalia jumping out of her skin.

'Joshua? What are you doing here? I didn't mean it like that. Sorry. Come in. It's been a long day!' She ushered him in through the front door and into the main lounge room.

'I'm worried about you. I needed to see for myself

how you were bearing up. If there's anything I can do, please let me know. Anything at all.'

'That is so kind. Really. I'm fine though. Still in shock, of course, but fine. I'm just so grateful that no one was hurt or…killed.' As she said that last word, the tears came unexpectantly.

Joshua instinctively put his arms around her. She was still in shock, and that combined with the sheer exhaustion of nonstop filming left her feeling vulnerable.

As he breathed her in, he loved how she smelt of snow and Winter jasmine, and how her long hair fell about his shoulders while they hugged. Joshua had wanted this moment from the first time he'd laid eyes on Mahalia Mason. If he could have, he'd had taken her right there. He held her tight, knowing that he might never get the chance to hold her again. Reluctantly, he lifted up his head from her shoulder.

'Where's Beau?' he asked tentatively.

'I don't know…we had a fight.' She sobbed again, her crying releasing months of pain.

Joshua wasn't sure if that was a good thing or not, so he just squeezed her a little tighter. She needed to cry, and he was happy to hold her while she did so.

Glad to be held, Mahalia sobbed for nearly twenty minutes. There were tears for her fight with Beau, tears for the fact that Margaret was on the loose, and in her mind, a dangerous woman; tears for Anita; tears for missing her parents; tears for the café. Tears. Just a lot of tears. Too many tears for one woman, she thought, but she was grateful for the strong arms and comfort that Joshua was so readily providing.

Beau walked through the door, and caught them both by surprise.

Mahalia pulled away, and rubbed her eyes. They were red and swollen.

'Where have you been? I've been so worried about you.'

'I can see that,' he said sharply, and walked to his studio.

'Does he always speak to you in that way?' Joshua asked once Beau was out of earshot.

'Never. That isn't him. He's probably upset to see me in your arms.'

'I best get going then. Please call me if there's anything you need,' he said. 'Promise me!'

'I promise,' and she pecked him on the cheek, then led him to the front door.

Mahalia paced the kitchen for ten minutes. It was wrong for her and Beau to be at odds. Was Margaret getting what she wanted once again? How dare he be angry that Joshua was hugging her? It should have been Beau holding Mahalia, telling her that he loved her; but no, all Beau offered her was his back. Had he actually walked away from her?

'Can we talk?' she asked, popping her head around the door of the studio.

'Is there anything left to say?' he replied, not looking up.

'Damn it, Beau. I can't live like this. Can't you see what she's doing? Once again, Margaret is trying to tear us apart. Don't let her! We're stronger than her.'

'You have absolutely no proof that it was her! I may not like the woman, and I certainly don't want her in my life, but that doesn't mean she's suddenly an arsonist!'

Mahalia didn't reply. She didn't have the energy for this. Space. She needed space to clear her head. The apartment was rented out. The only place to go was Limetree Hollow. It was a bit too close to Red Maple Manor for her liking, right now, but at least she'd only have to deal with her own mood.

'So that's it? You won't even discuss it? Fine! Have it your way!'

She packed a few bags of clothes, grabbed some food, and drove her pick-up down the snowy road. Tears slipped down her cheeks. If there was anything she was certain of in her life, it was that Beau loved her. If she didn't know better, she'd think he was on Margaret's side instead of hers. Why was he being so stubborn about this?

Cocoa

It was good to be back at Limetree Hollow. There were so many positive memories from her childhood here, and it always helped her to feel close to Granddad Jack. She thought of his wife, Ester, who had died many, many years before. Although her memories of grandmother were slim, like vague feelings that came up from time to time, Jack had kept her alive through his constant stories. Tonight, Mahalia was sure she felt her grandmother here with her. A soft hug in the night, a kiss on the cheek, a white feather falling from the sky. A whisper on the breeze: *don't give up, dear child.*

Mahalia slept fitfully, and kept her cellphone off. Beau could go to hell right now. Let him worry about her the way she'd worried about him all afternoon. Well, she assumed he would be worried. What if he wasn't? What if he didn't care? What if her accusations about Margaret were the last straw? They were stupid thoughts, she told herself. Of course Beau cared. He was being proud. Stubborn. Beau Candler was a man used to being in charge, and now he had to make compromises and work in partnership. He had to find his feet and learn a new way of being. If he needed time, he could have it. Of one thing she was certain: he'd have to make the first move. Beau would have to learn that pride was his enemy, not Mahalia.

At dawn's first light, Mahalia steeped herself a cup of chamomile tea and sat on the wooden veranda with a woollen blanket wrapped firmly around her as insulation from the chill. The beautiful sunrise made a mockery of her heart. The whole landscape of her life seemed so different now. Sure she had a successful book and a soon-to-be aired prime-time TV show, but without Beau, these things just didn't have the same resonance for her. What happened to the girl who was so self-content? What happened to the girl who didn't need anyone?

The shock of losing the café hadn't eased. Should she start again? She had the insurance payment to look forward to, and it would be more than enough to launch a new café. How could she afford to do that, though, and keep her valued staff on a retainer so they'd be available once building work was completed?

Slowly her thoughts turned to the cookery courses she wanted to offer at Limetree Hollow, and then the idea of being near Beau if their relationship couldn't be mended…

Life without him just seemed like an impossibility. She wasn't going to even entertain such thoughts. They were ridiculous. They were going to spend the rest of their lives together. For now, she had to stand firm and show him that even when they disagreed about important topics, she still loved him. Surely they could find a way through this? Margaret Pilkington-Candler, the thorn in their side, would eventually have to be plucked out. Together, they'd heal the wound.

Mahalia phoned the fire chief with her suspicions.

'Well, we can certainly get the police to question her. That she owns a Rolls Royce and is expecting a baby isn't exactly proof, Ms Mason. But I promise you we'll look into it. She's certainly the best lead we've got at this point, and given what else you've shared about her then we'll have to consider her a suspect.'

Would Beau despise Mahalia for telling the fire department about her suspicions? She had every right to tell them, she told herself. Every right!

As soon as she ended the phone call, her phone rang. 'Hestia? Hi. Are you okay?'

'Okay? Of course I am. I can't believe what Beau has done. It's so kind. Thank you!'

'What are you talking about?'

'The six-month salary.'

'What six-month salary?'

'Beau called me to gather the staff together yesterday afternoon. We met at the Emerald Tavern, and he promised to put us on his staff for the next six months, while you rebuild the café. We don't even have to work, we're on a retainer. He wanted to be sure we were all looked after, and that you'd still have us around when you reopened. But surely you knew all this?'

'No. No, I didn't.' Mahalia explained about her suspicions, and about Beau's jealousy of Joshua.

'Set me up with Joshua! He's gorgeous, and I'm more than happy to distract him.'

Mahalia laughed out loud. It felt like it had been ages since she'd really laughed. 'It's a promise!' She hesitated for a moment. 'I really had no idea that Beau met with you guys, and had arranged this. It's really so kind.'

'Yeah, he's a great guy. You got lucky there, Mahalia. Don't let him go.'

'I'll try not to,' she sighed.

On this icy-cold December morning, Mahalia rugged up, and brought some barrows of wood from the barn. The sooner she got the woodstove on, the better. She wondered if more snow was forecast. It sure was cold enough to snow.

Several loads of wood later, she carried a basket

of it from the verandah into the house. *Fire*, she thought to herself, *both a friend and an enemy*. She lit the match, marvelling at its power to warm and to destroy, and for a few seconds allowed her mind to become one with the flickering light.

It was only a matter of minutes before the heat dispersed around the kitchen. Even though she was in the mood for cooking, Mahalia knew better than to cook for one. She'd already gone up a dress size in the past week. *Discipline*, is what she told herself. *Stop eating cake every day!*

For three weeks, she didn't hear a word from Beau. Surely he must know where she was staying? Stubborn man! Three weeks! Mahalia decided that he took stubborn to a whole new level. She was damn well not going to apologise for blaming Margaret for the fire. Beau must know that she was right? Each day without him made her feel just that bit more uncomfortable. More than once, she felt a little ill at his absence.

Joshua phoned at least once each day, but she steered him towards Hestia, and his calls became fewer. It brought Mahalia satisfaction to know that even if her love life was doomed, at least Hestia's was blossoming.

Having time on her own brought clarity to Mahalia. She wasn't going to rebuild the café, or indeed, open a new one. And she wasn't entirely sure that she'd run cookery courses, either. The deep chill of Winter brought her other plans. For now, though, she would keep those to herself.

Chocolate cake. That's what I'll make today, she thought to herself. Mahalia fetched her apron from the coat rack, and pulled out the ingredients from the cupboard.

'Chocolate? Where are you hiding? I only bought a packet last week!' She groaned. The roads were icy, far too icy for her to drive to town. She didn't really want to go to the nearest shops just for chocolate, but the desire was pretty strong.

Eventually, she braved the cold and headed out.

It turned out to be a fairly pleasant trip, and she caught up with various townsfolk she hadn't seen in a little while. They were all thrilled about her various media interviews and were looking forward to the TV show.

While out and about, she treated herself to lunch at Tripper's Diner, and read the local paper. The editor was taking full advantage of her local celebrity, and devoted five pages to coverage of the new TV show.

'Famous girl!' Suzie Tripper said. 'You've made us all so proud! But we were so sorry to hear about your café. That's just too bad. By the way, haven't seen Beau lately. Hope he's keeping well?'

'Everything's great, considering.' Mahalia finished her sandwich. She didn't want to get into answering personal questions. 'Thanks Suzie. See you later.'

'Take care on those roads. They're icy!'

'I will,' she said, her broad smile beaming with joy at sharing some human company.

Jackson's Bend caught her by surprise, and within seconds she'd skidded off down the bank. There was no way she could back out of there. Thankfully she was unharmed, just shocked, and there was little damage to the truck.

'Damn it,' she yelled across the Winter's day, hoping someone would hear her.

It was an inconvenience she didn't need right now. No signal on the cellphone. Tears slipped down her cheeks. 'All I wanted was some bloody chocolate!' she sniffed into her tissue. 'Just chocolate!'

There was no other option: she'd have to walk the two miles back to the old homestead. Mahalia left most of the supplies she'd bought in the truck. All she took with her were necessities: chocolate, sugar, milk. Comfort. If she couldn't have Beau's arms around her, then she'd have hot chocolate. She had to admit that it was a poor substitute.

Despite her frustration, she quite enjoyed the walk home. The air was deliciously fresh against her skin, and it felt good to do some real exercise. Truth was, she'd felt rather sluggish lately, and knew she needed to do something other than cook and sit by the woodstove reading cookery magazines. It was a vicious circle, really.

While the milk heated on the stove, she sank into the sofa. That walk really tuckered her out. 'You're getting out of condition, girl. Better do something about it!'

Mahalia treated herself to a steaming hot chocolate, and decided to give the cake making a miss. Instead, she'd go for a walk up the hill. Not too far, but enough to work up a sweat and ground her.

After pulling on her woolly hat and coat, she ventured up the dirt track by the old well. Animals were hungry and scurrying through the woods in search of food: a red fox, white-tailed deer, and cottontail rabbit.

It was such a beautiful feeling to be back outdoors, that she couldn't believe how much she'd been in hibernation these past few weeks. Mahalia reconciled herself with the idea that she needed nurturing, and to tend to her emotional wounds. It had hurt her that Beau spoke to her so rudely when he found her and Joshua hugging. And why didn't he tell her that he'd been out all that afternoon organising to secure salaries for her café staff? Why was he so stubborn? Every part of her wanted to thank him profusely for his kindness. *Damn you, Beau! How can you do something as kind and generous as that, but not even talk to me?*

If it wasn't so cold, she could have stayed on the mountainside all day. Instead, she stopped for a snack before heading back to the house.

When Beau Candler drove back from his trip to Boston, he could hardly wait to pull into his driveway. Only another couple of miles until he was home. The incongruous sight of Mahalia's red pick-up truck tilted down a snow-covered ditch had him screeching on the brakes, risking his own life on the treacherous ice. Beau raced out to find her, but she wasn't in the vehicle. He could see she'd been shopping, and figured she must have walked back to the house. Beau grabbed her shopping bags and put them in his car.

Despite the icy roads, he drove as quickly as he could. What was she doing driving in these conditions anyway?

Immediately, he was alarmed to discover she wasn't at home. The fire was still warm, and there was an empty cup of chocolate in the sink. Where was she? Damn it, he said to himself. Things should never have got this far. Why was she so stubborn? And then he found himself laughing. She wasn't the stubborn one. *You're a fool, Beau Candler*, he said to himself.

As soon as he found Mahalia, he'd tell her that he'd been to Boston to encourage Margaret to get psychological help. He hadn't found her, but instead spoke to her parents and made provisions for her to be admitted into a prestigious mental-care facility. They were shocked and in denial that their daughter could do such things. At least Beau had tried. Surely that must count for something? When Margaret arrived back in Boston, her parents would take her there and she'd never be part of Beau and Mahalia's lives again.

Where is she? *I need you Mahalia*, he yelled. He was frantic now, pacing back and forward. Would she have walked back to town to get help? Yes, of course she would. Determined, independent; no, she wouldn't sit around waiting to be rescued. He headed out the front door only to find her emerging from the woodland track and heading towards his car.

'Mahalia,' he said, breathing a sigh of relief.

'What are you doing here?' she asked, taken aback by seeing him standing on her verandah. If it was possible for him to get better looking with time, then he most certainly had. He'd not shaved in weeks, but instead of looking dishevelled, she found him utterly irresistible.

'I'm sorry. I've been an idiot. You were right. I've tried to amend things. I've been to Boston to ask Margaret's parents to get her some therapy or something. She won't bother us again. I promise. Honey, come back home. I'm so sorry.'

'I don't know if I can. Home is a place where you feel safe...and I don't feel safe at the Manor when you speak to me rudely; when you don't trust me. Joshua was comforting me. It should have been *you* holding me that day, not him. Never him!'

Unable to look into his eyes, instead she looked down at her boots. How could she stay strong if she looked at him? Just one glimpse into his eyes had her forgiving him for everything. There was no way she could stay mad at him when her whole body just wanted to melt.

Beau stepped off the verandah and took her into his arms. With gentle fingers, he lifted her chin up until they were looking in each other's eyes.

'I'm sorry. It will never happen again. I promise you that. I was jealous of Joshua.'

'What do you think that he's got that you don't have? I really don't understand this jealousy. It's unfounded. I thought we'd talked about it? I thought it was resolved. It's *you* I love Beau, not Joshua or any other man. You. Only you! But, I would like to be friends with Joshua. He's a good guy, and now he's dating Hestia, he'll be in my life even more.'

'Hestia?' and a huge smile swept across his face. 'Of course you can be friends,' he said.

'I wasn't asking for permission!' she snapped, placing her hands firmly on her hips.

Mahalia was getting too furious for his liking. He'd have to default to the only tactic which worked: he kissed her. Not possessively. No, it was gentle, seductive, curious, tempting.

'I can't stand,' she moaned, as if her legs were about to give way.

'Good,' he groaned in reply.

And he swiftly lifted her off those feeble legs and carried her inside.

'I'm not making love with you,' she groaned between kisses. 'You can't do that every time you don't get your own way. It's not fair to disarm me like this.'

'Okay,' he said, and placed her down on the sofa. 'Call me when you want to come home, and I'll collect you. I'll get a tractor to pull your truck from the ditch.' And he started to walk to the door.

'Where are you going?' she asked indignantly. 'Just because I said I wasn't making love with you, it doesn't mean you can't stay, or that we can't talk.'

'I have missed you far too much to stay in the same room as you and be expected to keep my hands off you. I'm not that much of a gentleman! It's best if I leave.'

'Oh...' Her pulse was racing. 'Fine! Fine! You win.' She was exasperated, but she sure as hell wasn't going to be apart from him anymore. The past few weeks had been excruciating. 'I'm coming with you!'

But she didn't see the smile on his face as he walked to the car. And as she grabbed a few things to take with her, she didn't see him high-five the air. No, she had no idea just how darned happy and relieved he was that she was coming home. Finally, his Mahalia was coming home.

Winter kept them close to each other's arms, and it seemed as if they were kissing for the whole world. They had weeks of absence to make up for. Beau wasn't letting her out of his sight.

Spices & Secrets

Christmas Eve called to them with the flicker of candlelight, carols on the stereo, and the scent of cloves and oranges, inviting the lovers to hold the starlit evening sacred. Mahalia had gathered evergreens from the mountain, and decorated the mantelpiece and staircase, tying the branches securely with red-velvet ribbon.

Beau heaved a large fir tree into the lounge room, and together they decorated it with gingerbread star-shaped cookies.

'Wow. It looks fantastic!' she said, amazed at how something so simple could look so striking.

'Our first Christmas together,' Beau said, holding her hand tightly. 'And the start of many more.'

They were lured back into the kitchen by the scent of ginger, cardamom, cloves, nutmeg and cinnamon.

'Are you expecting a visitor,' Mahalia asked when the headlights came down the driveway.

'No. Are you?'

When the security lights snapped on, and lit up the vehicle, Mahalia's heart fell. 'It's your wife!' She let out an exasperated scream. 'Haven't those damn divorce papers been sorted yet? And...I thought she was going into therapy or something. *You promised*, Beau!'

'What the hell?' He kicked the chair. 'I'll get rid of her. Stay here.' Beau was furious.

'No, I'll get rid of her. You're too much of a soft touch when it comes to that woman!'

'Not any more I'm not,' he promised, his words firm. 'She's not part of my life, and she most certainly doesn't have a right to be at this house.'

Mahalia beat him to the front door.

'Merry Christmas,' Margaret said, walking into the manor without being invited. Her belly was full with baby; clearly due any time. Mahalia reeled. Oh my god, had she been right all along? *Was it Beau's baby?*

'No one asked you to come in here. We don't want you here, Margaret. You're not welcome.'

'I've come here to see Beau, not you. I'm here about our baby.'

Beau had joined them in the reception area.

'The only one here carrying Beau's baby is me. And I intend to have a peaceful pregnancy. Now LEAVE. Last warning. I never want to see you again, and nor does Beau. Let him move on with his life.'

'You're pregnant? To Beau?' Margaret's lip quivered. In that moment, she looked like a five-year-old girl, and ran out of the house, crying 'No, no, noooooooooo.' She was hysterical, and slammed the car door behind her. The tyres of her car screeched the length of the driveway, ripping apart the heavily laid white pebbles.

Beau and Mahalia breathed in deeply, shocked by her sudden visit, and then he laughed. 'That was clever, telling her you're pregnant. Giving her a taste of her own medicine, were you? Well done!' Despite the shock of Margaret's arrival, he chuckled all the way back into the kitchen.

'It was no trick, Beau. We're having a baby. And I'm sorry if that makes you feel trapped…it wasn't my plan,' she said as she busied herself with Christmas cookies.

'You're having our baby? Really?' His arms were around her, and while he tried to get over the shock, she turned around and looked up at him.

'You're okay about this?'

'Okay? I'm delirious! Is that why you didn't tell me? You were worried I wouldn't be happy?'

'On our first night together you said that children tied you to a person and that you were glad you hadn't been trapped with Margaret. I was scared that...'

'You're not Margaret. And I'm glad I didn't have children with her. But *you*? I want ten children with you!'

'Three at the most,' she laughed. 'Or else *I'll* feel trapped.'

'So you won't be drinking an Irish Cream with me then?'

'Afraid not! But I don't mind. It's actually rather exciting to have to think about this baby growing inside of me, and being responsible for everything I do. I just need to cut back on the chocolate cake!' she groaned.

They settled down by the open fire, and gave each other gifts, letting Margaret's visit become a faded memory.

'You don't think we should wait till Mom and Dad get here tomorrow?'

'No, this is nice. Just the two of us, having our first Christmas together like this. They won't feel like they've missed out on anything...apart from Anita, obviously.'

Mahalia was so touched by the sadness which crept across his face.

'Apart from Anita.'

They raised their glasses to an absent sister.

Mahalia carefully opened the small packet in her hands. She could tell by the feel of it that it was a CD.

Candler Ridge Christmas
20 Country Bluegrass Christmas Songs
By Lola Honey

'Oh my! Beau, is this what she's been working on so solidly all these months? It looks fantastic!' Mahalia cried to see that he'd used one of her photos on the cover. It was of Lola patting Carolina Blue, against a backdrop of fir trees and the old church house.

'Lola loved that photo so much she insisted on using it. I hope that's okay? Legally, I should have asked your permission and arranged legal documents.'

'Of course it's okay. It's perfect! She looks so beautiful, and the image is just perfect.'

'She's been a busy bee alright. Half the songs are ones she'd written herself. The others are covers. You'll love it!'

Mahalia opened the CD, and read the insert of the singer's acknowledgements. And then she read a note from the producer:

For Mahalia
I want the picket fence, the vegetable garden,
lots of children… and I want them with you.
Always loving you, Beau.

She laughed out loud. 'You're joking, right?'

'Do I look like I'm joking?'

'I can't believe you'd have that on the label, in print, for the whole world to see.'

'How else can I declare my love for you?'

'Just by being you! That's all you ever have to do. Don't you know you're my rock?'

A toot of the horn came from the driveway first thing on Christmas morning. Mahalia raced out to see her parents. It was bittersweet, that long, slow, rocking hug. Their first Christmas since Anita's passing. Together, they'd help each other get through the seasonal celebrations. The first anniversary of major events was always the hardest. Despite the sombreness which underpinned their reunion, Christmas day was spent with much laughter, an abundance of delicious festive food, and lots of singing along to Lola Honey's new CD.

Lola and her large Irish family came to visit later that afternoon, and the festivities continued well into the night with far too much Irish Cream consumed. Perhaps Beau knew it would bring healing to the family, to both families, as Lola's brother had died earlier in the year from an undiagnosed illness. Yes, they would all take the joy of Christmas deeply into their hearts, and move forward into the New Year with hope and happiness, and a sense of living life fully.

Mahalia loved how Red Maple Manor felt when it was filled with laughter and love. When she'd first arrived, she'd been struck by the beauty of the place but it had felt haunted, somehow, as if it was a mere shell of a building. Tonight it was a home; a safe place from the world.

The next morning, they walked to the church house in the snow, and laid wreaths by Anita's grave and that of her grandfather. They weren't forgotten. They never would be. There was no need for words. Sunlight shone onto the snow-covered graves, a symbol of life and hope. Hope is what moved her forward each day.

Red Maple Manor seemed so quiet after the Christmas festivities. Mahalia was shocked by how empty it felt when everyone left.

'I've changed my mind, Beau.'

'About what, my love?' he asked, feeling a tad concerned.

'Children.'

He hesitated. 'I think it's a bit late for that.'

'I don't want three. I want ten! This house is way too big to have any fewer than that!'

'I won't argue,' he chuckled. 'After all, I know how babies are made.'

New Year's Eve twinkled with delight, snowflakes falling, as Beau Candler bent down on one knee before Mahalia Mason in front of the blazing fire.

'Will you marry me, Mahalia? Will you live with me, stay by my side, and walk through the rest of life with me, for better or for worse?'

Too choked up to speak, all she could do was let her tears speak for her as Beau tenderly slipped a diamond ring onto her finger. 'Please say yes.'

'Yes, it was always yes. It was yes all those years ago. Of course it's *yes*!'

Beau scooped her up in his arms, and kissed her as if she was the only woman on Earth. And to him, she was. He'd love her until his dying day, and beyond.

As they lay in each other's post-lovemaking arms, Beau reminisced about her beauty, passion, and inner fire. He spoke about how he marvelled that she'd wanted to grow a garden, own a café, and be a mother. You're incredible. You do whatever you set your mind to. Brad was so wrong about you. You're one of the most sane, together, capable people I've ever met.'

'How did we get so lucky? Most people never experience a love like this, and everything about being

187

with you feels so natural. Except when you're jealous! Or when that horrid woman is around' she said seriously, and then laughed, 'I'm not entirely sure I deserve you.'

'Too late for that! You're stuck with me.'

'My parents will be arriving at 11am. Don't be intimidated by them. They're human. Just remember that,' he warned her gently. 'They're still coming to terms with the idea that Margaret and I never had a marriage.'

'Why didn't you ever tell them?' she asked.

'I didn't want to disappoint my parents. I'm the only son. It's a hell of a responsibility to carry the family name, to do things properly, by the book. And now I'm having a child with a woman they've never met. It's quite a thing for them to adjust to and accept.'

'Do you think they'll like me?' she asked nervously.

'I can't imagine anyone not liking you, but if they don't, then that's their problem, and I promise you'll never have to see them again. If they do, then I hope you'll feel free to welcome them into your life, and into our baby's life. But let's take one day at a time, okay? And besides, one mouthful of your cooking and they'll be as besotted by you as I am.'

Mahalia took that as her cue to head to the kitchen. Her belly was blossoming beautifully, and she loved how it felt when Beau's hands held her, touching their baby; making her feel like a goddess.

'We're having a baby!'

Beau headed off to his studio, and left her to potter in the kitchen.

For starters, she prepared lemon roast potatoes with aioli. As they baked in the oven, she set to work on the wild mushrooms, crisp-fried into a cake with chestnuts nestled on a bed of garlic-butter spinach and tarragon cream, and vegetables.

'You can not come in here when I'm preparing dessert,' she said as Beau looked curiously around the kitchen door sometime later. You and dessert are not a good combination,' she laughed.

'But it smells so good. I can't concentrate on my emails when the house smells like this. Surely you must have a spare spoonful I can sample?'

In a sign of submission, she raised her eyebrows. It was like this every single time. How could she argue with 'just a mouthful'?

And begrudgingly, she passed him a spoon so he could sample the rich chocolate and apricot liqueur. But of course it wasn't just a spoonful, no. It was several spoonfuls. 'You know, if you don't stop now there'll be nothing for your parents and that won't win me any favours.'

Abruptly, he removed the spoon from his mouth and threw it into the dishwasher.

'Honey, I think this kitchen was made for you.'

'Me too,' she grinned, delight filling her heart. 'I'm never happier than when I'm in here...' and then added, 'or in the vegetable gardens, or riding up the mountain, or in the churchyard, or at Limetree Hollow, or...' She was about to say the café...

'Do I come into this catalogue of happiness anywhere?' he asked curiously.

'They're all meaningless without you!' she laughed, not intending to omit him. 'They're here! They're here!' she squealed as their car crunched into the pebbled driveway.

'Don't panic. I promise they won't bite. Just be

yourself. Your gorgeous, irresistible, beautiful self.'

'I'm so nervous!' Her eyes pleaded with him to protect her.

Violet and Edward Candler stepped out the car, and Mahalia watched them from the kitchen. Well, at least they didn't look like monsters, she thought to herself. They surveyed the garden, in awe at how much it had grown, and the new flower beds under the snow that were obviously created by the lover in Beau's life. They looked at each other and smiled, and Mahalia felt hot tears spring to her eyes.

'Let's go out and meet them,' she urged Beau.

They walked, hand in hand, down the front steps towards them. Suddenly Mahalia found herself free of all nerves as she looked up and saw them both smiling so warmly at her. Despite their conservative natures, they reached forward and hugged her. 'Congratulations on the baby, this is such exciting news for our family. We couldn't be happier,' Violet said with a sincerity which touched Mahalia at the deepest level.

'Beau's a very lucky man,' Edward added.

'No Dad, I'm the lucky one.' Beau assured him.

'What is that gorgeous smell?' Violet asked as she walked into the manor.

'Lunch,' Mahalia said confidently, pleased that the aromas from the kitchen were already winning them over. Never mind food being the way to a man's heart, it was the best way to the in-laws' hearts, she decided.

'Do you eat like this all the time, Beau?' Violet asked her son in disbelief.

'Afraid so, Mom. It's such torture,' and he mocked being strangled.

'Stop it,' Mahalia laughed, tapping him with the wooden stirring spoon.

'My friend Channelle had been to your café several times, and spoke very highly of it. In fact, she says she planned her trips to Asheville based entirely on visiting the café. I'm so sorry about the fire, my dear. It's absolutely shocking.' She could tell that Violet was rather proud of the fact that Mahalia was about to become her daughter-in-law, and was deeply touched by her sympathy.

'Channelle? Long blonde hair, wears flowery long dresses?' Mahalia asked.

'Yes. You know her?'

'Her name rings a bell. She's an artist, right?'

'Yes!' Violet said, 'she says you were always so attentive to the customers.'

They enjoyed a wonderful lunch, followed by an equally delicious dinner, each of them confessing that they'd overeaten. Somewhere between lunch and dinner Beau had taken his parents for a walk around the property, pointing out new garden beds that Mahalia had created.

Once they settled down for after-dinner drinks, Beau played his parents a song he'd been writing. It was called *When Love is All You Know*.

'That's beautiful, honey. When did you write that?'

Mahalia had tears in her eyes. It was clearly a personal song about their relationship.

'The night you told me you were pregnant,' he smiled.

Edward wanted to know: 'Will you record it?'

'I had thought of giving it to one of my talent to

record, but I'm pretty attached to it, and have been thinking of putting out a small CD of my own work. It's just a thought. Nothing definite.'

'Honey, that's wonderful,' enthused Mahalia. 'Really wonderful. What's stopping you?'

'Nothing really, just not sure if it's the right time. We've had so much going on.'

All four of them looked up at the same time when a shadow cast into the room.

'*Margaret!*' Beau said, shocked by the sight of her with a newborn baby in her arms. 'What the hell are you doing here? You know that the terms of the divorce agreement include not turning up at my properties or making contact with Mahalia and I.'

'I just want you to meet your son, Beau. Is that too much to ask?'

Mahalia could see that Margaret was thriving on having an audience, and Beau's parents to witness the scene, and that she was about to milk it for all it was worth.

Was this nightmare of a woman *ever* going to go away?

'Margaret, please come with me,' Violet said, taking Margaret firmly by the arm and escorting her to the front door.

'One look at that baby and it's pretty clear just whose son he is! Ivan the personal trainer! Why are you here? Your life with Beau is over'

'But it *is* his baby,' Margaret insisted. 'We're lovers. We always have been. I just need that other woman to go. She's such a distraction!'

'Stop lying Margaret.' Violet was angry. 'You need help. You're a mother now; you can't play these sorts of games! I'm going to call your parents to come and get you.'

'No! Leave me alone. I just want Beau.' She pulled away from Violet. 'Beau! Beau!'

As her cries rang through the downstairs floor of the manor, Beau clenched his fists.

'Dad, promise me that you and Mom will stay with Mahalia till I get back? Promise me!'

'Yes son. Do whatever you need to do. We'll stay here.'

'What are you doing, Beau? Where are you going?' she cried, 'let me come with you.'

'No, honey. This is business I should have done years ago.' Beau kissed her on the forehead. 'You stay here and look after *our* baby. I love you.'

White with shock, Mahalia reluctantly let him go,. Even after all this time, Margaret was still intruding on their lives.

Out on the driveway, Beau caught up with his mother and Margaret. 'Go inside, Mom. Keep warm. Margaret, give me the keys. I'm driving you home.'

The smile on her face made him ill. Conniving, cunning, manipulative cow!

It was a long drive back to Boston, and they made the journey in complete silence, apart from when the baby screamed and they pulled over.

'Why aren't you breastfeeding?' Beau asked.

'Ivan didn't want my breasts ruined,' she said, looking out the window and avoiding eye contact with her newborn son.

'What a load of rubbish,' Beau said.

'And what would you know?' she hissed.

'It's obvious from the way Mahalia's breasts

193

have grown that what expands must contract. The changes to the breasts happen in pregnancy not during breastfeeding. Didn't they teach you that in childbirth classes?'

'No.'

'So, you're still seeing Ivan. Then why are you trying to pin this baby on me?' Beau asked.

'He…can't give me the lifestyle that you can,' she admitted.

'Finally, a bit of sanity!'

Beau continued to drive, furious at her deviousness and the way she'd slipped into his romance with Mahalia.

'Mahalia and I are marrying in the Spring. I need to know that we'll never have to see or hear from you again. You're not part of my life. The divorce settlement was more than generous. I can't give you anything else. I can't make myself love you. I have no interest in you. I never have. I'm sorry if that hurts, but you and your mother should never have railroaded me into marriage! And if you're honest, you'd admit that you never loved me either. I was just…a meal ticket.'

They stopped at a diner so Margaret could go to the ladies' room and heat the baby's milk.

Beau phoned Annie and Frank Pilkington. 'I need you to meet me at the apartment. I'm arriving with Margaret and her new baby. She needs help, and the baby is going to need family to raise him. Margaret is in no state to do this. She's unhinged. She needs you both. Please don't argue with me, and please don't go into denial again. You've fobbed me off too many times. Margaret will be going into psychiatric care as soon as possible. You can either be there for her, and support her, or you can pretend that this isn't happening. The choice is yours. But one thing is for sure. This baby needs a loving family. I have to go! See you at noon.'

Margaret strapped the baby into the car seat.

'Who were you on the phone to?' she asked suspiciously.

'A friend. Ready to go?' He was in no mood for conversation. Exhaustion had gripped him, and felt relentless.

'Yes.'

And again, they drove in silence. The sooner she was out of his life the better. Even though Beau didn't want her around, he had the decency to ensure that she was going to get the best professional help possible. It would be worth every cent for everyone concerned.

The maid greeted them at the door of their Boston home.

'Welcome home Mrs Pilkington-Candler; Mr Candler. Is there anything I can get you?'

'Tea, my dear. Tea,' she said pathetically.

Margaret pushed the pram to the lounge room and was startled to see her parents waiting there. 'Mom? Dad? I wasn't expecting you.' Immediately, she felt on guard. Had Beau called them here? And then her eyes caught sight of the man in the corner. Then she looked at Beau, and back at the man.

'What's going on Beau?' she asked, looking around nervously. She felt trapped, cornered.

'Mom, what's going on?' Her voice was high pitched now, and terror darkened her eyes.

'We're here to help dear. This is Dr. Jarvis. Jed Jarvis. He's going to help you get better,' she said kindly.

'I don't need to get better. I'm just fine! What's Beau been saying to you?'

She turned around to find that Beau had left the room.

'Beau, Beau!' she screamed. Within a second, her father grabbed her arms, and her mother took hold of the infant.

Dr. Jarvis moved in closer, and spoke to her calmly.

'Margaret, we're all here to help you. We're concerned for you, and for your baby. No one wants to harm you.' He spoke so tenderly, that she immediately calmed down. He seemed like a nice man, so perhaps he was going to help her. Maybe he'd help Beau to realise they were meant to be together. Yes, that was what he was here for! Nice man, she thought to herself.

Beau was in the kitchen, instructing the staff that their services would no longer be required. He offered them several months' severance pay, and asked if they could work till the end of the week tidying up the property.

'This house is going to be closed up for some time. I don't know when Margaret will be coming back here.'

'Mr Candler, we're so sorry. We had,' and the young maid continued, somewhat cautiously, 'suspicions for quite some time that things weren't right. I had actually tried speaking to Mr Pilkington, but he wouldn't hear a word of it.'

'I appreciate that. Mental illness isn't something people like to talk about or acknowledge. Thanks for all your years of service. I wish we weren't saying goodbye on this note. Of course I'll give you references of distinction, and nothing less.'

Beau could hear screams again from the other room. He felt sorry for Margaret; there was no question of that. But he felt more sorry for the baby who was about to be placed into someone else's care. And he hoped, with all his heart, it would be with the Pilkingtons; but he suspected they'd adopt the baby out. The shame of Margaret's actions would be too much for a proud couple like them. And when the police charged her with arson, the Pilkington name would be on all of the newspapers.

Beau left Margaret and her parents in the hands of Jed Jarvis and watched them depart. For an hour or so, he walked around his home and thought about the wasted years of his life: all those days and months and years of angry, but quiet, compromise. He wondered just what his life would have been like now if Mahalia hadn't turned up at Limetree Hollow. Not even for a moment could he imagine her not being in his arms, and waking up with her each day.

Beau walked away from the building that had once been his marital home, knowing that he'd never go back there again.

Exhausted from the long drive, he decided to stay overnight in a hotel, and drive home the next day, refreshed.

More than once Violet and Edward Candler put their arms around Mahalia. 'Everything will be okay, dear. Beau's just doing what he should have done a long time ago. Margaret needs help.'

'But the baby? Every baby deserves its mother. I can't bear the thought of it being taken away.' Mahalia began to cry. 'I don't know how I'd survive if someone took my baby away, and I haven't even met him or her yet.'

'Every baby deserves to be loved and nourished. Margaret isn't capable of that.' Violet sighed. 'You know, she was unstable as a teenager, but I can only see that now, looking back. Hindsight! I got caught up in the whole Pilkington plan for Margaret to marry Beau. If I'd stepped back a bit at the time, I would have seen that Beau wasn't interested in her. All my friends were preparing weddings for their children. I suppose, and I realise this isn't an excuse, I just got trapped in wedding fever.'

Edward said 'I've never seen Beau look as calm and content as he does with you. I don't know if I can forgive myself for all his wasted years. He didn't feel like he could tell us about the huge mistake he'd made in marrying Margaret. If he had, we could have helped to ensure a speedy divorce years ago. Such a waste!' Edward thumped the table.

'There's no point in regrets, Edward. We have to focus on what we've got now. What Beau and Mahalia and the baby have got now.'

'Thank you so much for staying with me. It means a lot,' Mahalia said, regaining her composure. 'I would have driven myself crazy wondering and worrying about Beau driving Margaret to Boston.' She told them about Margaret's visits: the first night, the horror of waking up in the dark to see her standing above them; news of the pregnancy; and suspicions about the café fire.

Violet gasped. 'You have to tell the police!'

'I've told the fire chief. I don't have proof. Just the circumstantial evidence of a Rolls Royce with a baby seat. It seems rather coincidental that my café would suddenly get burned down deliberately after all the features in the Boston press.'

'Of course it was her!' Edward said. 'I hope you'll rebuild the café and let all this nonsense be put to rest. She's not going to be able to harm you ever again.'

'I loved that café so much, but I'm going to be a

mother. That's my focus: nurturing and nourishing our baby. I don't want to be thinking about other people's wages, paying taxes, surviving food shortages after weather disasters, and the consequent price hikes.'

'Sounds like you know what you want,' Violet smiled. 'Let me get you another cup of tea. Chamomile, was it?'

Mahalia loved her future parents-in-law already, but she had no idea how very much they loved her, and thought what a perfect fit for her son that she was.

Beau arrived home utterly exhausted, and more than a shade guilty for his part in Margaret's admission into a mental-healthcare facility.

'You did the right thing, son.' Edward was firm. 'The right thing. She wouldn't have stopped until someone was killed.'

Mahalia shuddered at the truth of Edward's words, and gave a silent prayer that things had never reached that point. Images of her charred café came to mind, and a tear slipped from her eye. *Thank you*, she whispered to the Universe.

They spent the next few days with Beau's parents, comfortably getting to know each other.

'We'll be back in April for the wedding,' Violet promised. 'If there's anything you need, just ask.'

'I promise,' Mahalia said, her blossoming belly pressing into the baby's grandmother as they hugged goodbye. The magic of the moment touched them both. Violet reached to Mahalia's cheek and caught the tears. Without a word, they knew they'd be friends.

'Everything will be okay now. Just think about your baby.'

'I will.'

Edward hugged her in a way that she'd never felt before. It was a hug of love, friendship, protection, and mostly, it was of gratitude.

The Perfect Ingredient

It was the night before the wedding and Beau and Mahalia lay in each other's arms, listening to the birds of springtime whistling at dusk.

'You helped me come to the surface, Mahalia. I always felt like I was drowning, suffocating…but with you, I learnt to breathe again. You're right. Hitting rock bottom was the best thing that ever happened. And I wouldn't have truly known the highs of falling in love with you if I hadn't experienced the pits of being with Ms Pilkington. I don't want you to ever think for a moment that being married to you is a trap that I'm stuck in. I've never felt more free in my life than I do when I'm with you.'

A light snore came from her side of the bed; and he wondered how long she'd been asleep, and if she'd heard any of his declarations. Still, he could tell her again tomorrow and the next day…and the days after that.

Mahalia woke at dawn, and saddled up Carolina Blue. It was becoming increasingly harder to mount and dismount the mare due to her huge belly. She trotted down to the churchyard, and dismounted, leaving the horse to graze freely amongst the headstones and Spring wildflowers.

'Hey Anita. Hey Granddad. It's my big day today. I could never have got to this point in my life if it wasn't for you two. You held me, and you loved me, and you taught me so much about myself. Mostly, though, you let me be myself. Not many people have that in life. You both always accepted me, and my quirky ways. You never tried to change me, or control me. I wish you were here today, to stand by my side as I make my vows to Beau. I can feel you with me. I always feel you close by. I have a favour to ask. If you can hear me, if you really are walking side by side next to me, as I feel you are, please help me to be a good mother. I know I'll be a good wife. It's easy being with Beau, just like breathing, but I'm so scared of being a mother. What if I'm not good enough?'

Mahalia had no idea that just a few headstones away, Beau was listening to her passionate plea. He'd heard her slip out of bed, and didn't want her riding too far on her own. Tears streamed down his face. How could she even doubt for a second what a brilliant mother she would be to their child? She was such a natural nurturer. The way she cared for plants, people, and stray animals, and the way she created food to share: they were all indications of her ability to hold another human being. Quietly, he slipped away and headed back home. He had a wedding to prepare for.

The day hummed along at a quiet pace, with friends and family coming to the manor; caterers preparing for the evening meal; musicians setting up instruments and the sound system. Mahalia allowed herself to be pampered by the hairdresser, makeup artist and midwife.

The past year had been filled with such emotion, and such devastatingly life-changing heartbreak. There were times when she thought she couldn't put one foot in front of the other. Today was a new day. A beautiful day.

Beau had cracked her heart wide open, and she was certain that she wanted to spend the rest of her life with him.

Beneath the red maple trees, Beau stood surrounded by friends and family, including many names from the Country Music world. His gift to Mahalia was asking several of them to sing later at their reception. Keith Urban promised a rendition of *Making Memories of Us* as his wedding gift to them.

It was late afternoon as the Sun carefully lowered itself, like a woman whose belly was full with baby, from the sky down towards the horizon.

Today, Beau Candler would marry the love of his life.

The trees were strung with fairy lights, and a large silk marquee was set up in the parkland at the back of the manor. Caterers had prepared a feast, and the dining area was alight with beeswax candles.

Mahalia emerged from the manor, her arm linked with her father's arm, and stepped down the stairs. Her belly was huge, blossoming, and at seven-months pregnant, she looked radiant. If only her beautiful sister had been here to share her joy, she thought more than once.

The ivory lace and silk dress was classic empire line, emphasising the ample breasts of pregnancy, and her growing belly. There were ivory silk ballet pumps on her feet, and her hair was decorated with local wildflowers she'd gathered that morning from the churchyard.

'I have never seen you look more beautiful in your life,' he whispered when Mahalia reached his side. 'Truly, you look incredible. You always look amazing to me, but today...I can't describe it.' He shook his head in disbelief.

As Beau declared his vows before friends and family, tears slipping freely, he said 'there are not many things in life that we can be sure of, but this I know: you will be the best mother in this world. I've seen the way you care for animals, plants and people. If you can keep loving and caring for me even half as well as I know that you'll love and care for our baby, then I'll be the happiest man in the world. You've brought me so much. There are so many things I want to promise you today, but the most important one is that I'm going to love you like no one else possibly could. And...' he choked on his tears, 'and I know you only have eyes for me.'

Beau looked over to Jacob, his best man, and reached for the steel guitar that he was holding.

Mahalia recognised the song instantly, and tried not to cry. She'd heard him rehearsing it the other night, and had to walk away because it sounded so beautiful and left her in tears. There was nowhere to hide now. All eyes were upon her.

Beau sang the Lonestar song, *Amazed*. There wasn't a dry eye under those maple trees.

Her hand was on her heart, as if she could feel it exploding with joy. Tears trickled down her cheeks. Such lows, such highs in the past year, but right now, this high was the anchor to the rest of her life.

Mahalia wasn't sure she could say a single thing. It was one of her favourite songs, and she'd never heard it sung so beautifully nor with such meaning. And here she was, this day, surrounded by so much love. The vows she'd rehearsed, and the things she wanted to say, evaporated. In this moment, she was so overwhelmed. Overwhelmed by her undying love for Beau. She blamed the hormones of pregnancy, but it wasn't that. It was love. The feeling was too big for the words she'd planned.

There was gentle laughter among the crowd in acknowledgement. How could anyone speak after Beau's lyrical declaration of love?

'I'm amazed by you too.' She struggled to speak calmly, and to tell him how much she loved him. Mahalia was certain of one thing, though: she had the rest of their lives to declare her vows; the ones she'd spent a week carefully writing, planning, and making sure were just perfect.

'Beau, I've searched far and wide for the right ingredients to make the perfect recipe. All I ever needed was you!'

~ The End ~

Novels by Veronika Robinson

Mosaic
Bluey's Cafe

The Gypsy Moon Trilogy
Sisters of the Silver Moon
Behind Closed Doors
Flowers in Her Hair

Sweet Cinnamon Romance
Love at the Treble Clef Café
Love in a Scottish Storm
On the Wings of Love
Recipe for Love
House of Hearts

Moonlight and Motif
(magical realism novels publishing in 2023)
The Button Tin
The Soapmaker
The Irish Dollmaker

For a list of the author's non-fiction titles, visit
www.veronikarobinson.com

About the Artist: Heidi Harbers

Happiest when she's brightening up the world, whether it's decorating a room, painting a mural, growing a garden, feeding her chickens avocados, or organising fun events in her village, creativity is at the heart of Heidi's life.

As a pub landlady, and former restaurant owner, she has cooked for thousands of people across the years, serving up delicious meals, both traditional and unusual. When not cooking, Heidi's flare for transforming bare walls into canvases for her community to enjoy has earned her a wonderful reputation.

Australian born and raised, Heidi has travelled the world; and for many years has called England home. Born under the zodiac sign of Libra, the lovers, it is only natural that her art has found a home on the covers of romance novels.

Review Me

As an indie author, it would mean the world to me if you left a review of this book on Amazon or your chosen book retailer or book club. Thank you so much! My wish for you is a lifetime of love and happiness. ~ Veronika x